C000060100

Rules

For

Escaping

Stories

Nick Farriella

word west press | brooklyn, new york

copyright © 2022 nick farriella

all rights reserved. no part of this book may be used or reproduced in any manner without written permission from the publisher except in the case of brief quotations embodied in critical articles or reviews. for more information, contact word west press.

isbn: 978-1-7369477-1-5

published by word west in brooklyn, ny

first us edition 2022

printed in the usa

www.wordwest.co

art: hieronymus bosch (c. 1450 - 1516)

font: 'epicene' by klim type foundry (new zealand)

cover & interior design: word west

For my parents, Ligia and Anthony, who endured
so I could escape

Table of Contents

"The visible world is an imperceptible trace in the infinite revealed through suffering."

— **Yannick Haenel**, *Hold Fast Your Crown*

"This was to be forgotten, eliminated
From history. But time is a garden wherein
Memories thrive monstrously until
They become the vagrant flowering of something else
Like stopping near the fence with your raincoat."

— **John Ashbery**, "Suite" *Self-Portrait in a Convex Mirror*

A Big Break

What's happening now is my face is on the cool bathroom tile of apartment 2904 and my brain is being flooded with color. I'm not asking myself how did I get here or what happened because it feels like I've been here forever and this is always what's been happening. Color, all of it, at once, here in my brain like I had dipped my head into the paint mixing machine at The Home Depot, like the one I used to run for eight hours a day, the machine that spins like six cans at once, and I left the lids open, all four or five of them, it's happening here in my brain, all the colors flinging out and slapping against the plastic door of my thoughts.

I've realized I am immobile. Not rooted to the ground but suspended in a vast emptiness between floor and ceiling, which by now, I can't tell which is which; and the tide of color is receding, but I am floating in this state of stillness.

Did I take the drugs? No, not this time.

But, I will say: Entering Russo's party, I felt, how do I

say this, a bit off. Like my-head-is-filled-with-bees kind of off. And when he said, hey man have a beer, hey dude you want to hit this? I couldn't say no fast enough. Unlike me, at all. And so, but not really, I sat there watching Russo and Pucker and Tam play a card game with Jae and Ro-ro and Scams, flirting and touching and it was all so movie-like, like I was the camera, but also the director behind the lens directing them all with my thoughts. And I was like, that's it, hold your places. Now touch Scams' leg playfully, Tam. And he did. So, I sat back thinking, this is it, man, you know, like I've tapped into the river of reality, and I'm just swimming in it, free to splash or dive or whatever. So, I yelled out over the set, Break for lunch! And the cast and crew are just looking at me like I said a weird thing, so I got up and went to the bathroom. When the door opened, I didn't expect to walk into a garden.

I've been here since, face down in the grass, looking out across a vast plain of no hurting and no worries, just a slight tingling feeling in my arms and hands. You know, I'll tell you because you're listening, that what a relief this all is, because it's been hard, you know? Like existing? Like sleeping? Like concentrating on anything? So, for this big break to just come at this moment just goes to show that my coalition of molecules like means something in the universe... that I'm, like, connected and cared for. That regardless of the stresses that happen out there, outside this bathroom door, I will always have this pocket of the universe in my mind to escape to when things get really, really hard, and that's like what hope feels like or whatever.

Now, there's a knock, a voice saying, maybe yelling, "Leo! You cool?"

And I respond with my eyes, widening, pausing to admire the sun in the middle of the ceiling. I'm so cool. So cool.

Remain Open to It,
Without Naming It

Excitable Matèo Joseph, security guard, would be the first to enter the ninth-floor elevator of St. Peter's Hospital after having spent an hour hiding in the breakroom of the pediatrics department, secretly stuffing his face with superhero ice pops and leftover glazed Entenmann's Pop'ems. If ever asked by say, a future girlfriend—a total knockout, a busty blonde who is very much interested in his past life as an overweight security guard while lying post-coital in his mansion's grotto—whether or not he felt bad about once having stolen treats meant for sick kids, he had an answer ready to go: "But said treats are loaded with sugar, additives, and who hell knows what else," he'd exclaim, lathered and flexing. "And by denying sick kids of such toxins, am I not doing them a service? Like a hero?" He envisioned himself a hero. It was ten after eight in the evening, and he was buzzing from the sugar.

When he stepped onto the elevator, built in 1978, the shocks of the thing let out a brief scream under Matèo's weight. He sipped his iced coffee through a straw and pressed the button for the lobby. With the ding of initiation, he realized he was totally alone in this confined space—aside from the camera in the top corner of the elevator—and decided to start twisting his upper body slowly, whistling the melody to the beloved Christmas classic "Rudolph, the Red-Nosed Reindeer" while caressing the breast pocket of his stiff polyester shirt. It was July.

As the elevator started to move, Matèo made kissy faces in the reflection of the gold trim lining the wooden panels of the inside of the car and thought about how damn good looking he was and that if he wanted to, could hook up with any doctor, nurse, patient tech, patient, receptionist, cafeteria worker, environmental cleaning person, or security guard. So, what gives? Why the dating-app chats with over 80 total women and men that lead to nothing? He swung his ring of keys around on his index finger, rocking his hips to the beat in his head. Their loss, he thought. The elevator chimed as it reached the eighth floor. Doors opened; doors closed. Nobody entered.

Esme Cruz, charity care worker, turned over the deadbolt of the door to her fifth-floor office, then lowered herself behind her desk, holding a brown paper bag in one hand and a glossy pair of red rosary beads in her other. She was having a panic attack.

Matèo Joseph received a call over the radio to stop messing around. "You're on camera," the captain said. "Stop dancing in the elevator." He couldn't help it. He loved to dance. It was something of an anomaly, a guy that big being able to move the way he did. Six-foot-six, three hundred pounds; when Matèo got moving it was felt by all those nearby. Once, in a dance club, he had taken out an entire row of VIP booths just from shuffling his feet and twirling to Donna Summer's "On the Radio." When he went to radio back the captain to say something like, "You're just jealous, Cap," his radio made a strange noise, that of a dying baby antelope having its torso gnawed at by a full-grown baboon he had seen in a nature documentary. Ooh-wah. The battery had died. Just like the antelope. The elevator dinged at the seventh floor. Matèo kept dancing—his thoughts moving at techno music tempo.

Soon after hyperventilating into the bag, clenching the rosary, and repeating the prayer in Spanish, her breathing settled, heart rate lowered, and her vision aligned with itself again. This was Esme's third panic attack this week and she asked God why, why, why. The wine, God said in her thoughts. The four glasses of New Zealand cabernet sauvignon a night. Wine, a sin? She asked herself. Is such not your blood? No answer. It was under a doctor's orders, anyway, the wine. "Keeps the blood pressure down and keeps the mood up."

Matèo Joseph was really rocking now—heel tapping, arms shaking, head bopping; all that sugar sugar sugar flowing through him like electricity. Wah-hoo! Sixth floor, ding.

Still crouching beneath her desk, Esme noticed the polished red panic button encased in its silver box and felt inclined to press it. When the uniformed officer had installed it, he had said, "In case of an emergency," explaining that it triggers a silent alarm in the security console office and how an officer would be dispatched right away. During her first panic attack, she pressed it, thinking how nice it would be to be saved. But when the officer ran into her office with a confused expression on his face probably at seeing no signs of a threat or an emergency, just her, pale and breathing heavy behind her desk, she ended up feeling guilty. Internally, her body and mind were showing various signs of distress—racing thoughts, elevated heart rate, rapid breathing. But the officer must've not been able to tell from looking at her. A silent alarm, she had thought. That's what panic was. She decided to not press the panic button this time from under her desk, and waited for the feelings to pass by.

As she packed her things into her purse to go home for the day—another late night after a day of some volatile patients—she briefly considered the panic attacks to be a symptom of other illnesses in her life. Maybe it wasn't the wine. Things were rocky at home with her husband Paul; they were about to lose their section of the four-family home they rented from a gringo named Gerry.

Turning the lights off and locking the door from the outside, she also thought maybe it was her job that was starting to get to her. She'd been a charity care officer for twenty-two years now, approving or denying hundreds of thousands—if not millions—of people Medicaid or healthcare assistance; she felt like her job was a public service that she, an immigrant herself, was helping people get the medical attention they needed. And she was proud of that. Every patient she saw, for the most part, was so grateful to have the chance to come into this country and get some help. She knew what that was like, she had been there before—fresh off a small commuter jet from Colombia to Newark, walking down the tarmac for the first time to see what? Smog, industrial smoke stacks, bright colored advertisements for Coca-Cola, small law firms, Anheuser-Busch, and the Marlboro Man on a white horse, hung above large factories littered with graffiti—it was the 80s, baby–with cracked two-tone windows, ones if she looked deeply into she would see a group of brown people, like her, sweating on the line of machinery, hustling, hustling, hustling to turn out product after product. That was America to her, and it was terrifying. But also, kind of exciting. She didn't speak the language, but she knew a group of Latinas that found a community, a true slice of Colombia, in this small New Jersey town called Plainfield, where they had authentic panaderias, cafes, and boutiques. To her, it felt like she never left Pereira.

So, she understood. She knew how hard it was to find a

home in a new country, how opportunity for work, living, and health were mostly based on two things: luck and connections. Most of her patients had neither, so she didn't mind fudging some numbers, signing some forms, making some extra phone calls. But it was management that, due to pressure from their managers and their managers, and so on down the endless chain of boss's bosses, started to lower a heel onto Esme's department's neck—budget cuts, audits, patient credit checks. It became harder and harder to help her fellow immigrants, making her job more stressful, leaving her prone to feeling more tense by the time she got home, a tightness felt in a band around her head and a weight upon her shoulders, neck, and back. So to alleviate the tension, she would pour a little extra of that red wine, causing her to get buzzed and eventually drunk; drunk enough to argue with Paul over politics, identity, immigration and border control, and healthcare, and she would get this flushed feeling in her face from yelling her truth and Paul would say, "Calm down," and she would say *Callate la fucking boca*, because she hadn't been able to chill out since she left Colombia in 1978. And like the wine in her glass during a fresh pour, these thoughts would swirl and splash around her head, keeping her up at night in a cold sweat, quiet and still, but inside blaring and sounding off, the silent alarm of thoughts ringing and ringing.

Down in the security office on the lower basement level, five floors below ground, security captain Wayne Shultz unbuttoned his pants in front of the twenty low resolution monitors that he was supposed to watch for the next two hours; his console operator called out for the night and his relief got in at ten. When opportunities like this—privacy, alone time, no calls or codes to handle—present themselves, Wayne always thought it was best to take full advantage. He slipped his hand through the valley of his undone pants and under the waistband of his boxer shorts. Like a paid vacation. And with the more time he had to himself, the more perverse his thoughts.

Wayne Shultz was a retired state trooper, and now had no problem bossing around the young, twenty-to thirty-year-old security guards at St. Peter's for a decent salary on top of what he collected off his pension. So, with this financial backing and his take-no-shit-from-anyone Libertarian attitude, Wayne worked the job with no regard, doing what he wanted, when he wanted. What he wanted now, pants around his ankles while on Monitor Patrol, was to find something to focus on where he could grip himself like a bull rider and yank and twist and pull until the thing threw him off. So far, nothing. Just paunchy Matèo Joseph dancing in the elevator. He called to him on the radio and said cut the horse shit, that if he starts Code Blue-ing that he'll leave him there to die.

After Wayne ripped into Matèo, he clicked around the various screens in front of him, pulling up different cameras, controlling zoom and clarity with his mouse. A dumpster set against the back wall of the hospital had been ransacked by either raccoons or the local homeless gang known for expressing their collective views on late-stage capitalism in the form of fecal trash art. He zoomed in to see trails of a silhouetted stain on the wall, which he figured to be urination. He clicked over to the entry gates to the parking deck and saw a red Tesla leaving with the license plate "MGKHNDS" and knew it was driven by Dr. Nick Peters, resident physical therapist and racist piece of shit who had once muttered a slur under his breath when Wayne had handed him a parking violation. People hate to see a black man in a badge.

Wayne laughed in his chair, still touching himself, at knowing how much dirt he had on all the people who walked around this hospital like they were untouchable. Like, Esme Cruz, who he just saw leave her office with her tote bags, standing in the elevator waiting room, biting her fingernails. He was suspicious of her; she abuses the panic button in her office and leaves him with no other options but to send a responding officer into her office; usually only Matèo Joseph since his shift is so understaffed. He found himself thinking after every code clear that came over the radio, what exactly is this woman doing? In his four years on the job, she had rung that panic alarm more than any other department, including the psych ward. The late nights, the panic alarms—he suspected that she was tapping the young Matèo Joseph.

Thinking of Esme, he went soft. Not his type, beautiful curvy Latina women—well, women at all. He'd much rather prefer things, the more inanimate the object the better. Wayne was particular like this—never married, just had the police force, and was never interested in human connection. This obsession started when he was a rookie, working the evidence room for N.B.P.D. (New Brunswick Police Department) and he found himself spending his nights looking at nothing but plastic bags filled with stories. Not just any stories—juicy, crime-filled stories. Each piece of evidence, whether it be a bloody smashed TV remote where a woman had beat her husband to death with a dull hatchet, rusted over with dried blood and dirt from a friend attacking his friend, showed how people embedded themselves into objects. As he sat there, night after night in the evidence room watching over the bagged items, he found himself becoming aroused at imagining each person's spirit stuck on them; over time, the objects would change and his attraction would, too. This internal discovery had led to a shift in his perception; he would see people differently, seeing them almost the way they would see objects—bland, manufactured. Eventually he lost sight of human beings entirely, and only saw the objects they carried—bags, phones, clothes, accessories, etc. Sometimes it was sharp metal objects that got him going, other times it was glass, or steel, or plastic tech-gadgets. On his past few nights on Monitor Patrol, it had been architecture that did it for him—well-lit corridors, the empty waiting room of the Mother's and Children's Pavilion with handcrafted wooden arm chairs, a marble plated mantle above a glassed-in fireplace, and a green spotted medallion carpet, things like that. That's where he steadied the camera on Monitor 5 now. He was obsessive, not a creep. This desire, an itch; his toggling, the scratch.

The elevator's doors opened on the fifth floor. By then, Matèo was sweating from his temples and across his lower back; he decided to untuck his shirt. As he looked up, both hands forearm deep in his pants, Esme Cruz had stepped onto the elevator.

"Mrs. Cruz," he said, shuffling. "Hi."

"Oh, Matèo. Hi. What—" she said.

"I wasn't doing anything weird," he said.

"I didn—"

"Seriously. Think what you want. I was untucking my shirt."

"Okay."

The elevator dinged in response to Matèo double-tapping the lobby button; the doors didn't close any faster.

Oh, shiny linoleum, Wayne Shultz thought, hand going berserk. It would seem, that this new atrium—the one in the West Wing with sculpted marble archways over each entrance and the gold-filled joints of stone-tiled planters filled with philodendrons, palms, and ficus trees—was doing the trick. But just when Shultz was getting the tightening quiver of ascending release, he happened to glance over at Monitor 7 where he saw, of all people, Esme Cruz and Officer Matèo Joseph standing side by side in Elevator 3. What in the—He detached his hand from himself, only temporarily. These two, he thought, caught!

In the elevator, the two of them remained quiet. Matèo's fluttery sugar-hyper thoughts resembled some showtunes-like inspired blend of song and bird chirping, that if heard by anyone on the outside of his head would say, "Kid, maybe you should lie down." From his pocket, he lifted out a cold can of XSTREAM Energy Drink, cracked it open, and let the snake hiss inside for a moment before he tasted its venom. That's the stuff.

He looked at Esme and compared the darks swirls of her under-eyes to the toe of his smeared boot, which he hasn't polished in some time. She was standing there hunched, practically curling into herself. He knew her as the lady who cried wolf. Happened a few times. The first, he was mid-turkey, ham, and cheese sandwich in the Urology breakroom (they had cable TV) and the call squawked over his radio: *Brrrkaaaw.* "Panic alarm sounding in Office 511. Stat." He replied mouth full, garbling, "Okay, Cpt. Chicken. Yessirree," and sprinted into the nearest stairwell, down its taupe innards from floor nine to floor five, jogged to the office doors on the right—nope that way was 520-530—hightailed it to the other side of the wing, burst through the door of 511, huffing and wheezing and gurgling salvia to what? Nothing. This little old lady sitting behind her desk like a damn goose in the middle of the road, with squinty eyes, not saying anything, him just standing there idling in high gear unsure of what to do next.

Next thing he knew Esme was crying into his chest. He stood still, stoic, not saying a word. He felt that maybe words would have ruined the moment, so he let her cry until she was finished, then walked out without saying anything of it. The next day, she rang the silent alarm again and the same thing happened—they didn't speak, she just came out from behind her desk, tears running down, and buried her head into his chest. That night he went home and posted about it to an online discussion forum with a subheading of /weirdthingsatwork. Comments ranged from, "Dude, she wants to phuuck," to "That's really sweet and special, actually," which reminded Matèo that anytime he's found himself living in these extremes—either fucking or something sweet—he somehow ruined it by either asking what it was or trying to label it.

When Esme had rung the button a third and fourth time, he had understood it as their thing, as in something to share, which was fine—-like he thought, he could get with anyone in the hospital if he wanted. This old lady needed a big guy like him to cry on and it filled him with a sense of pride that his large, wide body was doing some good in the world.

But for some reason, his sugar amped mind didn't know how to react to her now, standing side by side in the elevator. Should he strike up a conversation? Ask her, Hey lady, why you crying so much? He figured that would ruin it, too, so he jittered a little bit more to the song in his head, Donna Summer's "On the Radio."

The elevator shook. Esme, who was now facing the doors as to not make any more eye contact with Matèo—it was too strange to look at the boy—took comfort in knowing there was a huge bottle of Cabernet Sauvignon waiting for her at home. She believed that's one thing the bible got wrong; the wine was the holy water. God forgive me, she thought. The elevator jumped again. She wished Matèo wouldn't move like that in here, big as he was, but she appreciated his energy and thought maybe that was the reason she was so drawn to him in her most vulnerable state, mid-panic attack. But now wasn't the time. She imagined the pulley cables snapping like ligaments. That reminded her—one of her patients today, a sixty-two-year-old rugby coach from Great Britain who needed reconstructive surgery on his ACL. He was a UK citizen here to coach some travel football team and tore every major ligament in his knee stepping off a smart scooter; so he ended up sitting at her desk in a boot, mad as hell. Mad at himself for ever getting on the thing, mad at America for allowing such an invention, but all that anger was taken out on her, like usual with her patients. He wanted the surgeries to be fully covered on America's dime, which sometimes would be the case for immigrants here on a work Visa, but after she ran his income check she found that he had near seventy-five thousand U.S. dollars in the bank and had to deny him any Medicaid. He responded with a few foreign swear words before hocking a missile of spit across the desk, hitting her in the cheek. Her hand flew towards the panic button, but she stopped just short of punching it. By then, the Brit was already out the door, so she sat there feeling the warm thick worm slink down to her chin. Part of her felt like she deserved it; she felt guilty anytime she couldn't help a patient.

What was he doing now, this boy? He was so strange, she thought. Constantly moving, tapping his oafish feet, shaking his massive hands. He must not have a care in the world. She glanced up at him from the sides of her eyes, thinking that maybe she should say something, but what?

Whatever it was about Matèo, maybe his size, Esme felt drawn to him in a way that she never was to Paul. With her husband, there was no communication, and she wondered if that stemmed from not speaking the same language when they first met. In the early days, most of their conversations were subtle looks and seductive gestures. It was all very sexy. Then she learned English, and that ruined everything. Eventually the only words they shared were bitter, condescending directives about money, politics, and the order of things. "Es, did you clean the floors? Do the laundry? The dishes? Es, iron my shirts. You spent HOW much on your hair?" This was why she drank: so his voice was less sharp.

Maybe it was the innocence she saw in Matèo, who now was looking at her with his mouth ajar, that let her feel accepted by him, let her think he wouldn't judge, ridicule, or turn her away—the acceptance of a child. And by leaning into him, she felt some sort of permission being transmitted into her that allowed her to feel free. When he held her in silence, she felt as if she were back home in Colombia as a young girl being touched by the strong wind that blew off the Otun River. Then she would spend her afternoons sitting near the bank and watching the men, one of whom was her father, drop large nets into the river and feel the thick, heavy humidity all around her as if she was being held by it. She often missed that—home, itself now a lost feeling.

Matèo shifted his gaze back towards the front and started nodding his head. Esme felt the floor stutter and gripped her tote bags tightly. Soon she would be home and have to see Paul. She wondered what he would say tonight to make her feel like an alien in her own home, a refugee constantly having to prove her worth to stay in his country.

As the elevator approached the first floor, thinking of Paul and her job, and trying to ignore a sense of longing for home, she felt her chest tighten, followed by a shockwave of a tingling sensation radiate through her nerves. The lights flickered, and the elevator shook before coming to a stop between the first and second floor. Esme felt stiff; her breathing began to increase.

As Matèo hit a few buttons, touched his radio, and went back to tapping buttons, Esme thought she had caused the elevator to stop running, that somehow her anxiety had manifested into frayed wires, a control panel on the fritz, cables splitting and giving away.

Standing up, leaning over the desk, Wayne was really in a sweat now; the heavy starched collar of his polyester shirt felt constrictive, chafing the back of his neck. He sighed at the beauty of the parking lot streetlight, innocent and laid out across the linoleum tile of the Mother's and Children's Pavilion. The blue glow of the monitors in the dim lit room was starting to mess with his eyes; they felt like small suns at high noon. As he pounded away at himself, he looked so intently at Monitor 5, of the geometric printed runway carper near the crystal glass sliding doors, he started to believe the souls of the objects were in the room with him, kissing his neck, whispering in his ear. Yes. You like that.

I've really done it now, Matèo thought. Given his size, he was used to breaking things, knocking things over in the tight bodega aisles, sitting on remotes, phones, laptops, tablets, etc. but an elevator was a first. It was stuck.

He tried to remain calm; he was after all, security. He checked his radio—still dead. He tried tapping a few different buttons—doors open, floor one, floor two, doors closed. No response. It was a 1978 Dover Traction elevator with mint doors that had no inner telephone system, only an alarm bell activated by a button on the panel. Matèo pressed this a few times; the clanging alarm made Esme flinch, but it didn't sound very loud, so Matèo was unconvinced that this would get anyone's attention.

"We're stuck," he said.

"How stuck?" Esme asked. She had backed into the corner now and Matèo could tell by the catatonic state of her face, similar to the one he'd seen when she alerted the panic alarm, that she was freaked out. He felt like he needed to save her.

His instinct was to shut his mouth out of fear that any more information would leak out, like about how he once saw a video of a guy who was stuck in this very same elevator car for a weekend before someone in engineering heard not the alarm bell, but him sobbing, covered in his own feces, or how right now Matèo needed to shit really really bad, thanks to all of the sugar that had hardened and sunk in his gut. He didn't want to induce any more panic in this poor woman. So, he sat down and tried to think. He listed his plans in his head as such:

A. Wave hands at the camera in the corner of the room until Captain Shultz or the console operator sees me.

B. Stand on the inner guardrail, that was gold plated steel rather than solid gold, and try to pop through a ceiling tile like in an action movie. Climb the steel cables to the top floor where I would be greeted by several busty blonds and television cameras.

C. Take busty blondes back to my place and—

C. Try to pull apart the elevator doors, also seen in some action movies. But after my intense muscle flexing, mouth wide, yawping rage as I spread open the heavy doors to probably find a brick wall on the other side and then yell, pounding my chest like a barbarian until, out of fear and the energy of raw human emotion, the elevator would kick back on.

D. If that fails, see how limited I am, even as a 6'6' 320-pound man.

E. Sit in the corner, tucking knees in arms, and cry, cry, cry.

F. Once found and freed from the elevator, change mode of behavior. Learn to see how precious life is—

it's not about busty blonds, becoming rich, XTREAM energy drinks, or dancing, dancing, dancing. There was something else. Maybe, possibly, human connection. Like what I silently feel with Esme. Seek that. Remain open to it, without naming or saying anything about it, but just feel it. A worthy pursuit for a hero.

Wayne was cramping now, losing grip of himself, standing on the rolling chair with one foot on the desk in front of the monitors for balance and position. It had never taken Wayne Shultz this long to finish; if anything, he prided himself at being a record-speed finisher at anything he did.

If his eyes weren't fixed on himself, now desperate to please just finish, he would have noticed in Monitor 7, Officer Matèo Joseph jumping up and down and swinging his arms at the camera, mouthing the words "Help."

In this state of aggression and panic, he felt like a slave to his desires. Knees quivering and wrist scorching, he felt so weak and powerless, he began to cry. It was there, in weeping and stroking, that he looked up to see himself in the reflection of Monitor 5, which had now gone dark from inactivity, and felt completely filled with shame. For once, the objects had failed him. Calls filled the console, voices over the radio came in, there was even a banging on the door, but he could not let go until he was finished, even if that meant his heart seizing up. But just as his heart-rate hit a spectacular, cardiopulmonary arresting rate, he glanced at Monitor 7 to see Matèo Joseph and Esme Cruz wrapped up in a loving embrace, causing him to let go of himself. There on the floor he wept, feeling as depthless as an object and longing to be held.

I am not my thoughts, I am not my thoughts, I am not my thoughts, Esme had told herself in the elevator. She had seen that mantra on Facebook. She couldn't really understand it, though. If she wasn't her thoughts, then who was she? This aging body? With skin that has gotten so white over the years? Was she her ethnicity? Born and raised in Pereira, Colombia? Or was she American, her identity of the last three decades? When holding these ideas up to inspection, they felt like nothing, and wondered what it even meant to be from somewhere and how that makes you who you are. Was she Paul's wife, his property? Was she an alcoholic? Could she be someone else? Her mind chased these questions around in a spiral that got tighter and faster the more she followed. Soon she felt so sunken into herself, she had no sense for the things happening around her; it all seemed muted and distant—Matèo jumping and flailing his arms, climbing up on the guard rail, punching the ceiling, jumping down, trying to rip open the doors, falling to the floor and resorting to curling up and crying into his hands. The marble ball of her anxieties slowly scraped around the inner track of her mind and felt like it descended so far down, she couldn't even see it anymore. It seemed ridiculous to try to chase it. What she needed while being stuck suspended in this elevator car, she felt, was what she had needed to do a long time ago—return home. She knelt to Matèo's level then helped him up without saying a word—that would ruin it—and then held him close, panic alarms sounding all around.

Three Times I've Seen My Dad Cry

1.

On a sunny afternoon in May 2006, I had skipped baseball practice to try psychedelic mushrooms for the first time; but when I got home to pick up the mushrooms from the basement refrigerator, I found my dad violently sobbing at the kitchen table. My first thought was that someone had died, maybe Mom, and I started to get the weak quivery knees and fluttery heartbeat of someone on the verge of tears. When I asked him what happened, he slid over a handwritten letter.

The letter was from a woman named Janice, she opened it by saying: *If this is Sal Farriella of New Brunswick, New Jersey who in 1976 struck and killed Cynthia Dixon with their car, please read on. I read on. I used to hate you.*

"Dad," I said. "What the fuck."

His head was in his hands, sobbing.

There were times when I tried to seek you out and ruin your life the way you've ruined mine.

But now, 30 years later, I forgive you.

"She just came into the road," he said. "Out of nowhere. I was on my way to the convenience store to get some mixers and cigarettes. Your mother had some friends over, it was around dusk."

"And you hit someone? Cynthia Dixon?"

"She was just a little girl. Six years old, I think. Just popped off the curb on her bike. I couldn't stop. I was 17."

I told him that I was sorry and that I hadn't known that happened to him.

"There were 5 witnesses, each said the same thing. Freak accident."

With her life, you took mine.

I wanted to sue you.

Later, my friend Sean and I agreed that instead of meeting up, we would eat the mushrooms on peanut butter sandwiches and instant message each other on AIM to document what we were feeling. It went something like this:

i feel sad

y?

my dad killed a little girl and i had no idea

r u tripping?

no
not yet
i dont think
but i feel warm

what about ur dad?

> i found him crying when
> i got home

weird
i dont think ive evr seen my dad cry

When the mushrooms hit, I felt like my body weighed a thousand pounds. I sat on the floor and left AIM up on my computer with an away message that said, "I am away from my body right now." I could hear my mom talking in the living room. I turned on the TV to a channel we didn't get. I couldn't believe that my dad could keep something like that inside for so long, and tried to imagine what that was like, carrying that around. Maybe that is why I felt so heavy.

Two years before then, when I was 14, we buried my cousin who had overdosed on heroin. I remember crying and crying, and at one point, crying only because I felt like that was what I had to be doing. Even though the weather was nice that day and the day before my tournament team just won States, and I honestly felt bored about the whole funeral thing, I cried to show my family that I understood what death was and how to take it, head down in tears. I don't remember my dad crying at all that day, because he was consoling me. Strange how witnessing a moment of weakness in him, I could see how strong he was, or has been. As I stared into the TV, I let the snow of the static swirl all around and consume me, thinking of my dad as someone who could swallow death like a pill, and let it dissolve until it burned his stomach, showing no signs of discomfort, the way men were supposed to, I guessed.

i dont think ive evr seen my dad cry

2.

The truck was filled with mulch; it stunk like shit. 96 degrees at 8 a.m. and climbing. August sun. My dad had made me help him fill the garden boxes and plant beds at the front of the house. It was 2011, a year after his brother's suicide. I was twenty-one, still living at home, old enough to technically be on my own, yet young enough to not know how to do that. I was still under his thumb, so when he needed help around the house, I had no choice.

My job was to fill a wheelbarrow with mulch and run it over to wherever he was so he could spread it evenly. I told him we could switch, that him being on his knees would be hard on his back, but he said to just keep bringing him loads. He didn't trust me with doing the most important roles of any job. We started having these broken up conversations while I was unloading the mulch and he started spreading. Usually we could only get one sentence in before the wheelbarrow was empty and I'd have to go back to the truck for a refill.

You see the game?
Yeah, Yanks suck
I'd come back with another load.
They have no pitching, I tell you.
No hitting either.
I'd go and come back.
You see that guy on the news? Guy from Piscataway. Ex-chief of police.
The suicide by cop?
The barrow remained empty. He stood up, squinted into the sun.

Yeah. Fucked up. Had his wife and kids in the house as pretend hostages.

No shit. Why'd he do it?

Why does anybody do it?

I went to get another load.

While I was dragging clumps of mulch into the wheelbarrow with a pitchfork, I thought of my uncle's life and tried to map out things that made sense for why he took his own life. He was broke. Alcoholic. Pancreatic cancer spreading into the stomach, liver, and kidneys. But these points weren't so obvious; they didn't really add up to a definite suicide. If I looked closer, I found less relevant things about him that could have contributed: Depression. Divorce. On the verge of going back to jail. And if I looked closer than that, I still found things orbiting there around him that could be factors: Lost mom at 12 years old. Rage issues. Possible bipolar/obsessive compulsive disorder. I figured that's what suicide was, a culmination of an infinite number of traumas, piled together like grains of mulch until it all got so heavy, you could no longer break it up, compartmentalize it load by load, and move it to somewhere else to spread it out where it all felt real thin, and things like flowers could still peek through and not be suffocated by it.

From the stereo speakers hanging outside of my dad's woodshed, I heard the opening chords to "Simple Man," by Lynyrd Skynyrd. I filled the wheelbarrow to the top and rolled it across the lawn to where my dad was, hunched behind a bush of Azaleas. He was sniffling.

Hey.

He walked up to me and hugged me.

I miss him too.

31

3.

Winter, 2014. It snowed the whole time we were on the road. We almost crashed, twice. My dad was driving frantically, wild with impatience. My mom kept checking her phone in the front seat. The energy in the car felt like there was heavy metal blasting, but the radio was off. I was distracted, having just broken up with my girlfriend, and was looking forward to getting to Long Island to forget about having been cheated on, at least for the night.

My sister was in the Mothers & Babies Unit of Good Samaritan Hospital, having complications with the birth of her daughter. The baby's neck was being squeezed by the umbilical cord; she wasn't due for another two and a half weeks. The cord was wrapped around her neck four times.

My mom had gotten a text from my brother-in-law saying that Anne was being rushed into surgery and that we should come up as soon as possible. We threw ourselves into the car, my dad in his New York Football Giants pajama pants, my mom with a skin healing facemask still on, and me half asleep from working a double shift at the warehouse that morning. It was Christmas Eve, too.

We sat in bumper-to-bumper traffic on the Belt Parkway. My dad slammed his fists on the steering wheel, my mom chain smoked with the window all the way down. The cold air found its way into the backseat and woke me up a little bit. I tried distracting myself by looking out the window, watching what else was happening in the world. My eyes followed people as they crossed the busy streets of Queens carrying grocery bags and walking fast, probably on their way to their big, warm family gatherings. People hung around outside of convenience stores with their hands over their mouths blowing smoke. Stereos played loud Christmas music. Cars honked idly, for no good reason. In every person I saw, I pictured a life better than mine, even though I knew that wasn't possible. Each of those people had experienced loss, or would experience it, but I envied them for not being right in the middle of the uncertainty of it. I thought about what if my sister was losing the baby or worse, what if she was dying, and looked to my parents for answers in their faces. All I saw was wild, raw fear. But as the traffic picked up and soon after the lights of the city were blurring past me, I only saw focus; in their determination, I read an un-denying certainty that everything would be okay.

We got to the hospital just as my sister was out of surgery. She and the baby were fine. My dad let heavy single tears drop one after the other from his right eye. I liked to imagine that each tear was filled with grief, worry, stress, fear, and trauma; and that after he wept, he would be relieved of it all. My niece was born at 5 lb. She smelled like mozzarella cheese. In the recovery room, we laughed about that until we cried together, as a family. When I looked over at my dad as he hunched over my sister holding the baby, I could have sworn that he looked freed of some weight, like he was floating up towards the ceiling.

Analogia Entis

1998. It's August. There's hardly anyone on the beach. The morning sky hangs low and overcast, creating coins of light flipping on the ocean's surface. The sun seems further away than usual. Under it all, there are two fishermen sitting beside their rods that are being held up by two pieces of PVC dug into the sand with a red cooler box between them. Their lines disappear out over the greenish water. A sharp gust whips off the dunes. One of the fishmen has a fat lip of chewing tobacco. Both are drinking light beers. They stare straight ahead. A stone's throw away from where they are watching their lines, a woman holds an infant close to her chest. It doesn't make a sound. The other fisherman lights a smoke. The blanket in which the infant is wrapped waves like a flag. There is a light mist in the air. It's hard to tell if the woman is crying or not; she swipes at her cheeks. Her blistered feet dig into the sand as she walks toward the shoreline. Sandy Hook is known for its rocky and shell-filled foreshore. From where they are sitting, the fishermen can make out the edges of New York City's skyline through the distant fog. The woman is now near the break. The fisherman who's smoking says to the other fisherman that he's been having a rough time, a crisis, feeling like lately he's having a real lack of faith. The other fisherman stays quiet and spits tobacco out onto the gray sand. The other takes a long, serious drag from his cigarette and while blowing out smoke, tells the other that it's been like he's been walking around with quicksand in his gut; that it's been this nonstop sinking feeling there ever since the clock hit midnight on January One. The other spits again. This time the tail-end of a loogie blows and hangs off the seam of his jeans and he asks, do you believe in omens. The other draws from his cigarette and says nope. Well, The Spitter says, once I woke up from a nasty dream where my mother had cut her own eyes out with a dull, two-inch long Santoku, right in front of me as if I were a mirror, and when I woke up I had this real weird feeling in my stomach where it felt like acid just sloshing around in there, and I thought nothing of it other than maybe I drank too much the night before or something, until the phone rang sometime later and it was Dad breathing heavy and talking all slow trying to tell me that Mom has been diagnosed with stage five glaucoma. He spits again, then says, after that I've always been real mindful about feelings in my stomach; that somehow, maybe, the stomach is connected to a world we can't see, and intuition, he points to his gut, and insight, pointing to his head, are tools to two different realities. They both continue to stare straight into the choppy tide. Seagulls loom overhead. The woman lightly tiptoes back toward the cove she came from. She is visibly weeping. The blanket hangs freely over her shoulder. The wind blows. The fisherman who's smoking notices a heavy tug on his line. Clouds completely engulf the sun, as if it's being stubbed out. None of them will ever forget this day.

***

1995. A woman is feeling nauseous on an airplane. Curls of cigarette smoke hang above the cabin. Outside, the plane passes through dense clouds that remind her of mountains. For a moment, she forgets that she is off the ground. Below, the ocean reflects the sky and vice versa, giving her a feeling that she could only think of to call *revuelto*, or Topsy-Turvey. Her child blinks at her from the window seat. The man next to her is looking at her lips. He is not her husband. The captain mumbles something in English over the intercom. Her knees begin to shake. The man next to her shuffles in his seat. A stewardess passes by with a short skirt also the color of the sky, just like her little hat; she is taking drink orders. The air on-board is stale and hot. Somewhere a baby cries out. The cabin jolts as if on skis. Her child blinks and taps his little hand on the armrest between them. The cabin shakes again and starts its descent. The woman in her seat now begins to pray. The man next her reaches over and caresses her thigh. Her eyes tighten. The child stares at the spotted puzzle of the man's hairy hand. The captain announces, Bienvenido a America.

***

Marlon Reed, of Justice & Reed Restoration, fixes his tie in the vanity mirror in the crammed back bathroom of the shop located on the corner of Vesey and Church. His eyes feel dusted shut. He's just returned from a meeting with a Bank of America loan officer on the eleventh floor of Tower One that was interrupted by loud alarms and frantic directives to exit the building immediately. He found it strange that upon pushing through the front entrance doors into blinding light of the end of summer sun, he was met with plumes of dust and what felt like buckets of water being thrown in his face. The air was thick with chalk, so it was refreshing. At the sink, after persistent splashing of water in his face, he finally clears away the crud that seeped in his eyes as he was walking back to the shop. When he looks again at himself in the mirror, he realizes that he is covered in blood, not his own. He hears what sound like explosions in the street. The television says, we've been attacked. Marlon can make out tiny specks flailing down beside Tower One and raises a tentative finger to the dried blood at his temple. He has no idea where Daron is.

***

On a winter night in Charlotte, a man is dragging a Christmas tree down the block, creating a wake of brine in his path. The speaker strapped around his neck blares rap music audible up to the second-floor apartment window where Julian Cruz and James Reed look out and watch their breath blur out their faces. The man with the speaker walks up and down their street daily, sometimes up to four times back and forth to the liquor store on the corner. They call him "Beat-Bop." City lights dot the black veil of sky in the distance. It's their last night in town before Winter Break '09 and they are passing a joint back and forth.

"So, you think you'll take the bus?" Julian says.

"I think I'll think about it," Reed says.

"Wait it out, yeah."

"It hasn't even started snowing, yet."

"And yet, we have plows."

"I can't believe I have to drop out," Reed says.

Julian lets his statement hang there.

A motorcade of four trucks roll by; their plows scrape the pavement. Julian notices a film strip of orange boxes sputtering along the window. He is thinking that he wants nothing more than the sky to open up and bury the town in snow.

They are roommates, often confused for lovers. After the joint burns too low to hit they shut the window and turn on a movie. It's a war comedy and extremely violent and very funny. After the movie, Reed tells Julian that he thinks the film industry is dead.

They light another joint and bicker over Reed's use of the word "dead."

"Like no signs of life," Reed says. He has low, thick eyebrows that move up and down when he talks.

Julian tells him he's being an inexorable douche, that every day there is something good being put out into the world.

"You're so overzealous."

"Purist," says Julian.

"Look, I get it. Joe Schmo's across the globe now make cool art films on their iPhones and put it up on their YouTube page for 7 views or whatever, and they're actually probably pretty good, like better shit than a young Kubrick. But all I'm saying is that they aren't industry."

"So, they have to be 'industry' to be relevant is what you're saying." He doesn't even burn him on saying "Joe Schmo's."

"I'm saying hitting a hundred homers in a minor league season doesn't count."

Julian walks away into the kitchen and puts on a pot of coffee. He looks at his reflection in the frost-bitten window. He is wearing a hoodie that somehow makes his nose look longer. Through the pane, he spots heavy clumps of snow falling in spirals and sticking to the street. Everything seems to be going as planned.

***

The scene at the beach on June 17, 2002, is pictur-
esque. The humidity of morning has burned off, leaving
a smooth plane of blue out over the water that bears re-
semblance to the visage of an iris as far out as one can
see. A red flag flaps idly next to the lifeguard post where
an overly tan young man stretches his back, flexing his
greased muscles. A pack of three young women nod in
unison to a boombox nearby and pretend not to notice him
under big, dark sunglasses. The shelly foreshore is mild-
ly crowded with groups, some families, and some couples
laying out on towels, some in chairs under striped um-
brellas, and others mingling about throwing frisbees and
footballs, etc. etc. Off to the side, near a low, grassy dune,
a young boy of about ten sits by himself and begins to dig
into the sand with a small orange shovel. His face is contorted with a pout. No one around seem to notice. There
is a determinism in the way he digs, like he wants out, like
he is digging as some sort of revenge to his family, who
also don't see him from where they are sitting on a beach
blanket, looking out to the glassy ocean, unwrapping
homemade turkey and swiss sandwiches. He digs and digs
until his plastic shovel clunks on something hard. The ice
cream man swings his bell at the planked entrance of the
alcove. Kids run right by where the boy is digging. He
reaches down and pulls out a wooden box, then drops his
shovel and runs over to his family. His stepfather is shoo-
ing away a flock of six or seven seagulls that are plotting
to steal his French fries. The boy hands his mother the
box. The sun is directly overhead. Jesus Christo nice find,
she says, dangling wooden rosary beads over the box in
front of her face.

***

Yo, yo, yo, my mans, my mans, stop, yo, for real, just, yo, yo, stop, says Beat-Bop in the street being patted down by a police officer. Julian Cruz looks on from the storefront window of Kindle and Burns' Puzzle Emporium. In his hand, he is shifting around the Perplexus, a 3-D marble maze inside of a glass dome. He can hear the sleet falling off the shingles and plopping on the sidewalk. The shop is empty. His shift ends at three. As the police officer takes the man with the speaker down to the pavement, the phone rings. It's Reed, he had to wait out the storm for a later bus.

"I'm thinking of how many ways there are to die again."

"Would you care to list them out?"

"Let's see... just getting out of bed this morning," Reed says. "Cerebral aneurysm, ST segment elevation myocardial infarction, faulty dry wall screw anchors in the ceiling fan, cryptogenic stroke, carbon monoxide poisoning, burglary, black widow spider bite."

"Okay, too far. Are there even black widows in North Carolina?"

"Do you think you can feel an aneurysm coming on?"

"You're stressed. It's Finals."

"I'd love to see the statistics in how many accidental deaths of college students there are during testing weeks."

"Are you implying that stress can manifest itself in obscure, and by the way, extremely rare ways for a young person to die? Hang on."

"Is that a suicide pun?"

The bell over the door rings and the police officer is standing there scanning the store. The windows are blurry and foggy from the cold rising off the wet ground. Julian asks if he can help him with anything, and realizes he is still holding the Perplexus.

"What's that?" The officer says.

"It's a marble maze, essentially."

The cop's nametag says K. Markson. He asks if he can see it and Julian hands it over, then goes back to the phone behind the desk.

"My stomach feels like lead," Reed says.

"Have you called Shainey?"

Dr. Shainey O'Rourke, LCSW, offers college kids free therapy in exchange for weed.

"No, but I talked to my dad. He called, saying all the plans are in order for me to take over the shop. He said I hav—"

"Hey, is this thing even possible?" Markson shouts, shaking the Perplexus.

"Yeah," Julian says. "Just try to think ahead. Get creative a little. Think outside the box."

"That's your advice to me having to drop out of college? To you never seeing me again? Think outside the box? Maybe you're having the stroke."

"Not you, Reed," says. Julian.

The cop is getting more hostile with the Perplexus.

"And so," Reed says on the phone. "I was like but how could I possibly come live in New York. I feel so crammed there."

"Yeah," Julian says. "At least we have some real mountains here. Escape."

"Then he said he needs help in the shop, that they are struggling, blah blah guilt guilt guilt."

"Hey," Markson says, now at the counter, standing across from Julian. "I need to get a statement from you, what you saw happen in the street."

Julian says to Reed he has to go and will be home soon and notices the smashed Perplexus ball sitting on the counter; the cylindrical orange finishing cup had been removed and has the marble resting in it.

Markson shrugs. "I thought outside the box."

41

***

James Reed hates his father for being cold and dismissive his entire life but still couldn't say no to help him with a new flyer for the restoration shop. It's the end of summer, nearing the first-year anniversary of the day his father started to drink. He is sitting at the kitchen table in the Bayonne apartment. He is twelve. A breeze passes through every five to eight minutes or so. Pills of light stripe the river. The skyline still looks void of something, the way an amputee must feel. James wonders how long that feeling lasts as he colors in the block lettering of the words, "Restoration Sale: Families of Victims Only. Starting September 1st."

***

"I, Julian Cruz, am nothing but a collection of cells that change completely every seven years."

"I, Julian Cruz, am nothing but—this is stupid."

"Say it," Reed says.

"I, Julian Cruz, am nothing but a collection of cells that change completely every seven years."

"Again," says Reed.

Julian repeats himself.

"And I, Julian Cruz," Reed says. "Will not judge myself based on the actions of those old cells, because I have compassion for those old cells, that know not what my new cells know."

"Oh, for fuck's sake, dude."

"Julian."

"It's bullshit."

"It's not."

***

The street outside of the Charlotte apartment is bustling with speeding cars and the distant whirring of air condition units. It is muggy hot. Griddle hot, Reed's mother, Jalisa says. They just brought up the last of his boxes and furniture. Outside, the distant echo of rap music comes and goes.

"Still don't know why you chose Queens College," Marlon Reed says, dabbing his forehead with a wet paper towel. "There's only two seasons here. Hot as fuck and cold as fuck."

"Marlon," Jalisa says.

Reed ignores it and hears a knock at the door. In walks Julian, a tall brown skinned kid with both of his ears pierced with fat rhinestones and a funny haircut that's shaved on the sides and floppy up-top. His t-shirt can't hide the faded colored lines of a cheap tattoo on the inside of his biceps. He shakes Reed's mother's hand first then his father's, finally Reed's and says, call me Jules.

"Where you from?" Asks Marlon.

"Jus' bout a stone's throw away up yonder past Gastonia."

Later, on their first night as roommates, where they rigged an apple into a one-hitter and got so stoned in Julian's car Reed thought of the Carolina stars as a low-hanging canopy collapsing on him, Julian laughs about not being able to keep up with the fake southern accent anymore.

"Wait, what?" Reed asks.

"I'm not from here," he says, in no accent that Reed can't place at all. "I just live here. I was born in Colombia. Moved around a bit since. Boston. Jersey. Virginia."

Not even the wind could wipe off Reed's smile.

***

"What's up with him?" Says Carly from next door.

Reed is hugging himself and shivering, pale white, and rocking back and forth on the floor of the common room of Oak Hall.

"Finals," Julian says.

***

After the third day of the visitors, his mother says the house is cursed. Julian is ten. He calls them the visitors because they come at night and wake him up, three tiny goblin-like spirits dressed as Mariachi men marching around his bedroom. When they come, he feels hot and tense and breathless. They are so vivid, like made of green fire, and so intense, their laughter makes him cry. After night one, he tells his mother, I figured it was just a bad dream, and after the second time, I figured it was because I was thinking about them all day long, but three nights in a row... Julian's mom, Esmerelda, twists her lips and gives him a quizzical look. She tells him that for the past three nights she has had intense nightmares about an old man spirit who stands over her bed, waits for her to wake up, and tries to strangle her. Julian cries in his mother's lap.

The next day Esmeralda goes to the market with her acquaintance Elaine, whose family has been in the neighborhood for four generations.

"You're in the blue-shuttered Victorian over on Forest, right? The three-family?"

Esmerelda nods.

"Oh, well, you know with any of these old homes. Could have been a murder, a suicide. That stuff lingers."

Esmeralda swallows a heavy lump in her throat and

adds two more tomatoes to the hanging scale. The cold mist of the produce section feels good on her newly sunburned neck from the beach the other day.

***

"Car accident, stray bullet, crushed by bails of telephone poles off an eighteen-wheeler, hit by falling scaffolding, grand theft. Rabid dog. Lightning strike. Trip on uneven pavement and crack skull."

"This is just something he does?" Leo, from 905, asks Julian.

"And that's just walking down the street?" Julian asks. "What about snorkeling?"

***

The relationship between Julian and Reed is one of luster and confusion. The kind of suppressed masculine love that expresses itself through witty banter, red-faced argument, and the occasional drop-everything-wrestling-match to prove who is better when words begin fail them. It's childish, but it's real. It's the kind of relationship that is founded in control. One that could last a lifetime or explode any day now. There's a certain codependenc, especially for Reed, who needs Julian around in the morning to start his day, make his coffee, and slowly transition into function with some back-and-forth, sports replays, shooting the shit. Without it, Reed is irritable, moody, down.

Julian is seventeen.

Reed is nineteen.

Julian is the son of a Colombian immigrant, his mother. His father, in his mother's words, was, "the Holy Ghost." Julian was born in Pereira—a modular city planted right

smacked-down in the middle of the Andes mountains—
and moved to the U.S. when he was about three. It was
just him and his mom in a tiny, slightly haunted Somerville
apartment, north of Boston, until he was almost ten, when
she got a job in a plastics factory outside of Plainfield, New
Jersey. His stepfather, Frank, was her shift manager. Soon
after, they moved into a three-family home that had a flow-
er-woven arbor over the front entryway and ghosts in the
attic.

Reed is the youngest of four brothers, from American-born
parents. Born and raised in Bayonne, New Jersey. When asked
about his ethnicity he says, in a sort of dance, "A little bit of Czech,
a little bit of Pol, a dash of Italian, some Irish, a little bit of this, a
little bit of that. I'm a mutt." Being the youngest, Reed never got
the attention that a first or second-born son would normally get.
There is such a thing as too many trophies. "Probably out of sheer
exhaustion," Reed once told Julian. "My parents let me get away
with anything."

They fell into friendship extremely fast, seemed bonded by
the second semester of their first year, spending late nights in the
library or dorms, taking shots of cheap Russian vodka, talking
or sometimes simply staring at each other in thought. Their
relationship has a tinge of homosexuality, a hint of attraction,
the kind that playfully encourages the other to be at their best,
but never to the part of sexual curiosity; they both unabashedly
straight, maybe deeply deeply closeted.

They challenge each other intellectually. Reed is more of
a realist; Julian, an idealist. Reed's arguments grounded in
facts and statistics; Julian's in intuition, art, and sometimes
spirituality.

Julian's dependency on Reed lies in his need for a male
role model, someone to fill the father-shaped void inside of him, even if he is only two years older. He thrives
on Reed's encouragement, his attention. He depends on

Reed's weakness to make him feel strong. Where Reed looks to Julian for emotional support, his mirror of reminding him that he still exists.

All of this is completely unknown to the two of them, of course.

They are men.

***

"What's the worst thing you ever done?" Reed asks.

They are in their usual place near the window. It's September of their second year. Reed's head is shaved. He keeps running a clammy hand over the scalp, as if he can't believe it's gone. Julian is lying back on the floor, resting up against a yarned pouffe. It's still summer hot.

"Um. Hm," Julian says. "When I was kid, I would pee in the corner of my room."

Some seltzer dribbles out of Reed's mouth.

"What the fa—why?"

"Laziness mostly."

They both laugh and then Reed relights the end of his joint that had gone out.

"But come on," he says. "That's like not even that horrible."

Julian says okay what's yours and tries to think more. Reed tells him that one time at a party in high school, this kid Steez that everyone picked on was wasted out of his mind and at first it was pretty cool cause he was just dancing like an idiot and making them laugh, but then it got pretty bleak and Steez confessed to the group of guys that he wished they were dead, that if he could buy a gun, he would blow them all away.

"I mean now I can understand," Reed says. "We picked on him kind of a lot."

And so, Reed continues, the guys had just laughed it off almost, like okay psycho, and the party went on, but later, on the way back from the bathroom Reed had found Steez passed out in a room, just all alone, face first on the floor with his ass in the air.

"I shouldn't have said anything," he says.

Next thing, Reed says, the guys were huddled around Steez and handing Reed this empty beer bottle and chanting.

"You didn't," Julian says.

Reed slides both of his hands over his shaved head and leaves them there for a second. When his face emerges, it is beet-red.

"I did," says Reed.

"You shoved a beer bottle up some guy's ass?"

"What made it worse," Reed says. "It shattered when he jolted up and fell on his back."

***

The TV says, "Aren't you DYING for a new television? You'll DROP DEAD at these low prices." It's ten o'clock. Tomorrow is Christmas Eve. Dense clouds are breaking up. A handful of stars collectively popping. There is no music coming from the street. Reed is still visibly shaking and hasn't said a word since lying down in the common room a few hours ago. Julian sits above him on the sofa and pats a cool, wet washcloth around his face. He notices his lips are bluish with white cracks. When Julian looks deeply into Reed's irises, he sees a murky green tide receding into black. He clicks off the TV. Outside a car passes and the sound of its tires passing through the flooded street sound like glass breaking over and over and over. Julian feels as though he is losing control of the situation.

***

It's the Thursday before Fall Break '09. The sun is a white pool in the center of their living room. The songs of birds are being pushed out by Beat-Bop's music from the street. Reed just confided in Julian what his father said to him before starting their second year. They are sharing a cigarette in the window.

"He said that?" Julian asks. "That if you don't get a 4.0 this semester, he's pulling you out?"

"The shop is really struggling," Reed says. He ashes out onto the garden box.

Julian notices tension in Reed's forearm, notices the grip he has on the cigarette.

"So, what does that have to do with you?"

Reed tells Julian that he wouldn't understand, that he wouldn't understand trying to please a man to no avail, to want someone to look at your life and say you did it, say they are unbelievably proud. That Julian is lucky to never have to know what it feels like to never be good enough to a person who is biologically conditioned to love you.

"Do you know what that feels like?" Reed asks. "Like never-ending cardiopulmonary arrest."

"I do," says Julian.

***

Julian is perched atop his mother's house in Plainfield and has large, dirty white angel wings. He is watching someone in the street. Sometimes it is his mother, sometimes it is Frank, but mostly it is Reed. Julian watches as Reed walks down the sloped driveway and into the street, around to the driver's side of a tan sedan parked at the curb. Always, before Reed opens the car door, Julian swoops down

49

to the street and kneels before Reed and lets him rip out his wings feather by feather until he is bleeding out from two gashes in his back. Julian has noticed that he never cries or screams, and that he awakes with a strange notion that he deserved it.

***

Outside the hospital on Christmas Eve, from the view from the tenth floor, Julian notices the way the sun splashes right up against the heavy gray clouds and disperses shards of light around to the thinner, papery clouds and across the windows of nearby buildings. It's probably going to snow again. He can't stand the constant beeping of Reed's heart monitor; it's like each one pricks his chest. When Reed wakes, Julian gives him some lukewarm chicken noodle soup from the cafeteria. Julian points out how he looks like a baby bird.

"I feel chewed up and spit out," Reed says.

"I'm sorry," Julian says.

"It's not your fault I got so stressed out that I had some sort of episode, some cytokinetic storm of bodily responses. That's another one, by the way."

Julian lifts the pillow behind Reed's head and pours him some more water. Reed says he doesn't remember much since missing his bus home for winter break and his dad calling him, that it's all pretty much a blur since the night they got snowed in together. Pellets of precipitation fleck against the window.

"Thought of one. Anesthesia overdose."

"How do you live with yourself after doing something horrible?" Julian asks.

"Define horrible."

"Unethical. Immoral. Sinful. Shameful."

"I've been thinking a lot about this story my dad once told me," Reed says. "He once told me when I was real young how he used to get premonitions or something, and that one day, while fishing with his old business partner Daron, a woman had dropped her baby in the ocean."

"Holy shit. Like on purpose?"

"Yeah. And that, before that, he had this nasty stomach pain that whole day, that whole year basically, and all of sudden, while explaining his stomach to Daron, his line got hooked on it, the baby, and they had to untangle the line from its neck and—"

"Fuck."

"No, but they saved him. My dad and Daron saved that baby. And so, I've been thinking a lot about how that morning affected them and like rippled through their lives in so many ways. It was after that my dad and Daron went into business with each other, and they both looked at restoration as some sort of good deed, a service to society. That it was an honor to uphold antiques and memorabilia for people trying to hold onto the past. So, a good came from that bad morning."

"So, you're saying that you don't believe in horrible acts?"

"I'm saying, I don't know. That I wouldn't be so sure to call one out right away."

"What about Steez?"

"He moved away after that. His parents sued the shit out of Rodney's parents, whose house it was, and made near seven figures in compensation. I think he ended up at M.I.T."

"What about how when Daron died, your Dad started drinking heavily and converted the shop to only restore objects of only 9/11 victims' families and then he became so entrapped in this want/need to help these people by restoring their memorabilia, that he realized that by making changes to their stuff, it is no longer their stuff, that a fireman's ax with a newly sanded handle and replaced head is no longer that same fireman's axe, driving him to near suicide, to the point of ripping his son out of college just to propel his delusion?

"Or what about if you were around the age of three and can vividly remember the saliva hanging off a stranger's lips as he fingers your mother on an airplane, and you did nothing except pretend not to see?

"Or what about if you were ten and you were at the beach with your mother and your stepdad and you couldn't take hearing your non-father's laugh and seeing his ugly yellow teeth, so you went off and just started digging and digging until your shovel hit something that made you stop digging. It was like a treasure, but a curse—"

"A curse?"

"So, what does that mean? What does it mean when something appears to be a treasure but ends up a curse? Those rosary beads I found at Sandy Hook that day caused these hauntings, inexplicable coincidences. My stepfather got ill; my mother had these vivid nightmares; I saw these little green spirits. I can't remember what they looked like but it was like a terrifying parade, they grinned and laughed at me while I hid under my blankets, and all this went on for three or four days, up until my mother brought the beads to a priest and had them rinsed in holy water. So, what does this all mean?

"What does it mean that you would put grinds of poisonous mushroom in your roommate's coffee on a night where you thought the snow would take care of cancelling his trip, and you watched over a two-day period as the poison flowed through his blood stream until attacking his nervous system, causing him to have a nervous breakdown, all so he will stay. All so he will stay here with you and stay in school and far from his crazy, abusive father?"

Reed just blinks. "So, are you saying you believe in curses?"

***

Dr. Shainey O'Rourke, LCSW folds the little plastic baggie and stuffs it into the inner coat pocket of her scarlet blazer. She is without shoes, dangling her right, bare, foot over her left knee. Reed notices dim slits in the cloth in her undershirt where, if he tried, could probably see through. He's not trying. The carpet has a dense pile height and a faded medallion print. There are two acrylic lamps on both sides of the accent chair where she is sitting, dimly spewing light through round cream-colored drum shades. Even though he is actively not trying, he still takes account of how freckled she is. The sun is being muted by heavy lavender curtains behind her. Dr. O'Rourke tells him they have an hour. It's the first day of the spring semester.

Noose Tattoo

—for Mad Dog

When my uncle showed up at my door unexpectedly, he had a noose tattooed around his neck and carried a long rope bundled up in his hand. Over the few days he lived with me, he'd toss the rope over the counter when coming in the door. He'd sling it over his shoulder out in the yard when doing what he called "Jail-aerobics;" propane tank bicep curls, cinder block shoulder presses, push-ups with his feet three stairs up. When I said, "Uncle Frank, what's up with the rope?" He said something about casting his own judgment, that the rope was a reminder. "Reminder of what?" I asked. He lowered the collar of his shirt revealing that crazy tattoo.

"That we're born with our heads in the noose," he said.

On Monday, I called my dad and told him about Uncle Frank's tattoo and that he's carrying a six-foot rope around with him.

"When did he get out?" he asked.

"He just showed up on Saturday," I said.

"Keep an eye on him, will you?"

"He even lies down with it stretched out next to him on the couch," I told him, "Like a snake."

The next morning, I awoke to the smell of pork roll and heard it crackling in the pan. There was Uncle Frank, shirtless and completely tattooed, leaning over the stove, rope wrapped like a scarf around his neck. He asked how I slept. I asked if he did at all. He held a can of beer in his left hand. It was 6:45 a.m.

"Hey, I got the paper," he said. "Read me the front page."

I read him the front page of the *Times*, some story about the governor getting locked up for tax fraud. He let out a manic laugh and said, "He's not going where you think he is. He's going somewhere with tennis courts."

"Is that where you were?" I asked, kind of joking.

"No," he said. "I was in a hole."

He clicked off the burner and scooped up the pork roll, egg, and cheese and slapped it on a split bagel on the counter. He took a sip from his beer then dropped the plate in front of me and said, "For you." When I asked what he was having, he lifted his beer, smiled that jack rabbit insane smile, and said, "I'm good."

It was Tuesday. I had to call out of work from my late shift at the warehouse to give Uncle Frank a ride to a meeting with his parole officer. The meeting was at two o'clock, so we spent that morning digging trenches in the yard to lay some ties down. Frank wanted to make a garden. When he showed up a few days before, I didn't know what to think; he was always carrying some unforeseeable hook with him that came around when you didn't expect it. Like this past Thanksgiving. He had disappeared all afternoon, missed the Giants game and everything. We started dinner without him. He turned up halfway through, burping and stinking of the bar, salt and pepper shakers spilling out of the inner liner of his jacket, cackling and red-faced. He told me to follow him out back, that he got something for me. It was a new Huffy mountain bike with shocks on the forks. He was so proud. The elation of the gift carried over into the living room where we watched the highlights of the game, ate pie, drank some beers. I thought things would be okay for a while. That maybe this time, he'd stay for good; he'd get himself a job and would be my uncle. Until there was a knock at the door and Uncle Frank fled to the basement like a dog in a storm. It was the cops. He had stolen the bike; plus, he had warrants. They took him away with pie cream still on the cusp of his mustache. So, when he turned up again, out of the blue, talking about building a garden in my backyard, carrying that long rope, I didn't reject the idea that something was coming up right behind it, some bitter harsh reality coming up on its tail-wind. I joked in my head that maybe he needed some place to hide a body.

Near the George Street exit, Uncle Frank told me to pull over. He had the rope twisted around the entire length of his arm. I asked him what was the matter. He said that if he went to his PO meeting, he was going to get locked up again—he owed $1,200 that he didn't have and they were going to test him for alcohol, which would be like testing his lungs for air. I had a decision to make. His hands were shaking in his lap. I watched the panic rise in him and course through his veins up to his neck as he took quick short breaths. He squeezed the end of the rope with both hands.

"Yeah, the noose is getting tighter," he said. "I can feel it."

I didn't know what to do. Trucks blew past, making my car rattle. For some reason, in that moment, I remembered something that my dad once told me about Uncle Frank. It was after my tenth birthday party. Someone stole all the cards with the money in them. Everyone blamed Uncle Frank because that's the kind of guy they took him for. Tattooed, biker, drunk. After they accused him, he left the party, went to a bar, got roaring drunk, and laid down his motorcycle going 90 miles an hour on the turnpike.

His handlebar ripped through his spleen. On the way to the hospital in my dad's truck, he said, "My brother has been paying for his sins with his body his entire life." That really stuck with me, cause every time he'd show up, he'd have a new injury to report—a bum knee, broken fingers, missing teeth. My uncle's body was a tableau of reconciliation, except often, it wasn't his own sins he was paying for, it was his family's. I never did tell my dad that a week after that, I found my birthday cards in my cousin's car, with no cash in them; I think he had used my birthday money to shoot heroin.

I decided to not drive Uncle Frank to his parole meeting. I said, fuck it. We kept going on Rt. 18 all the way to the shore. He turned up the radio, Black Sabbath was blaring. He drum-rolled on the dash and let out dog calls: ow ow owww! He even tossed the rope into the back seat. I thought maybe he had some sense of freedom back, which I felt pretty good for giving him. I couldn't knowingly drive him to that meeting; it would have been like arresting him myself and dropping him off at the prison gates.

In Asbury Park, he asked me to stop at a liquor store. I said, cool, and asked if he needed money for some beers. He said, "You kidding? I'd never take money from my nephew."

He was in there a while, so I smoked a cigarette outside of my car and watched two crows walk along a telephone wire. They were the biggest crows I ever saw, and they moved in tight unison, back and forth, beaks bobbing. I had the feeling they were watching me, conspiring. Perhaps, it was me feeling guilty for breaking the law and technically aiding a wanted criminal. I thought, taking long drags of the cigarette, what if the cops were able to use birds for intel? Just use some sort of chip that makes them track and report crime. So, I looked up at them and flashed my middle fingers. I said, "Fuck you, crows."

My uncle rushed out of the liquor store with his hands in his pockets.

"What, are you talking to birds now?"

We got back in the car. I put on my seat belt and backed out of my spot, looking both ways. Uncle Frank said, "A little urgency please." It was then I realized the store clerk rushing toward us waving his fists in the air. I sped off.

"Frank, what the fuck? You just rob that place?"

"Borrowed," he smirked, sliding a few tall boys of Natural Light and shooters of Jim Beam out of the inner lining of his denim jacket.

We went to the beach and got drunk. The weather was shit, since it was April, but it was nice to have it all to ourselves. Heavy clouds rolled over. The sea looked chaotic and angry. The sun came in bursts; one minute it was there, the next it wasn't, and all was cold and gloomy. We sat near the jetty, drinking and smoking. Uncle Frank told me stories about his days with the Hells Angels, running guns and crank. What a life. I threw French fries at seagulls. It was the best damn day I ever had with him. I figured the memory of that day would stick forever. He was so much like that sparse sun, that when he came around, you had to appreciate the shine and warmth of his presence while you could. He was kind of electric like that, full of energy. I told him that I felt pretty bad about not taking him to his meeting.

"What's going to happen next?" I asked.

"Another warrant, probably."

"You know you can't stay at my place anymore, right?"

"I know. I never stay in any place for more than a few days, anyway. You take care of that garden."

I told him, I will.

A strong wind came over the beach. It was bitter cold and whipped up sand in our faces. The problem with memory is that I'd like to imagine he was crying instead of wiping the sand out of his eyes, because if I saw some tears, that would have been an inkling to the sort of pain he was in. Instead, I couldn't see shit, just sand.

We drove back with the radio off. He kept to himself, not saying much, just staring out the window, watching the signs on the parkway blow past. I wondered what kind of movie was playing in his head. I hoped it was something nice, like those old westerns he used to love and made me watch; the ones where the bad guys always got away. I thought he would figure something out, he always had.

He told me to drop him off at Edison train station, so I pulled right up to the awning to let him out. It was raining. He gave me a hug and told me to take care of myself. He said, "Thanks for a great day, nephew." When he walked off, I rolled down the window and yelled, "Uncle Frank! You forgot your rope."

He turned, and said, "No, I didn't," tapping the tattoo around his neck.

The next morning, I awoke to a phone call from my dad. He asked if I saw the news and told me what happened. The moment was framed. In it, I could smell the faint iodine smell of fertilizer and fresh cut grass wafting in through the window. There was the sporadic chirping of birds, and roars of truck engines in the distance. My thoughts slowed down; my heart increased. The beauty of spring felt repulsive. Time sped up again. We were in the living room, my parents, my aunts, some cousins. It was night and we were watching the news, waiting for it to change, to say something different; we watched it over and over, and it still said the same thing. Man struck by train in New Brunswick. Once news is news, it never changes; it becomes something else, not a memory or even a report, but something solidified, hardened in time, inaccessible and something removed. I searched endlessly through Twitter on my phone, hoping to get some inside scoop, but only found people saying who ever caused commuter delays deserved what they got.

The family had a wake and a funeral, and no one knew what to say. My aunts made up reasons for why and my cousins didn't want to talk—instead, they took shots of Jameson in the parking lot of the funeral home. That's the thing about suicide: it's like a bomb that goes off in a family with shrapnel blowing through the rings of whoever was close enough to feel the blast. No one knows how to cope. The survivors are left removing shards of guilt and anxiety from what is left of their defenses, trying not to bleed out, with one lingering question: why? I knew why. I told myself the noose around his neck got so tight, he felt like there were no other options. I always thought my uncle would be the type to chew threw the rope and find a way, but the noose was a part of him all along, like the damn tattoo.

After it was all over, I told my dad about our day at the beach. He said it wasn't my fault.

"I know," I lied.

Then I sat on the porch of my parent's house, smoking cigarettes, and watching crows take off and land on a telephone wire. Nothing and everything had changed.

Unhumanness

When he arrived at the tennis courts for the first time, Leo knew it to be a desperate act to end his recent bout of what he called *unhumanness*; that if experiencing things through your senses and interpreting them into a collective of emotions and actions is what makes you human, then human he was not. Lately, when met with an onslaught of awfulness online, instead of engaging in some sort of call to action of voice or opinion, what Leo felt was the mental equivalent of an endlessly slick and glossy bowling lane—his thoughts just rolling over themselves forever. In a way, he hoped this, tennis, would finally be the thing that redeemed the parts of himself that seemed lost, or gone, pieces of his soul now so diluted he felt they were maybe never there to begin with, that his habits online had boiled the bones of who he was down to this murky broth of emptiness. He did, however, keep some aspects of himself. Anxiety, the fucker, for one, has always been there. And his God-given athletic ability. Even though he never played tennis before—he grew up playing what his father deemed "men sports," football, baseball, and hockey, which all leave you swollen and stupefied—he figured how hard could tennis be, people in their seventies did it. It would, he hoped, save him from swallowing himself whole.

61

###

Leo was back living at his parent's house, something he wrangled and twisted into a lofty tale about redirection, about financing, about it being a strategic lateral move, part of the plan, instead of what it actually was: a last resort. He had fucked up, royally. The gory details of his swift departure from his uppity corporate job and gated condo living were murky and shameful at best, liable at worst. He wanted to spare his parents from any implication, legally or morally speaking, so he just told them painful change was necessary for growth. How could they push back? Any parent knew that to their core.

Barb and Gene were retired, so they had all day long to monitor the premises, to scan the searchlights of their eyes, keeping the thirty-year-old prisoner to his designated areas: the basement and the kitchen. But even there, he wasn't safe from interrogation. Coffee turned into mock-interviews. Laundry, a defense strategy. In passing, an orderly shun. He felt it necessary to stay out of the way, anyway. He looked at their routines as if he was watching some boring, glossy sitcom. Every day it was coffee in the sunroom—Gene, a paper. Barb, her iPad playing some word puzzle game. This lasted until midmorning, where they split after breakfast until lunch. What they did in the privacy of their separate offices, he hadn't a clue. Dad probably slammed the libs anonymously on the Internet or jerked off to the endless scroll of high-definition porn he had missed out on his entire adult life. Poor guy. Mom, he imagined, took various video calls with relatives, maintaining some semblance of responsibility to loved ones that was obliterated by social media and texting, or maybe she chatted with some guy in Latvia, who sent her heart emojis the way her husband never could. Leo didn't know; anything was possible. These people were no longer his parents. These people have done away with his parents, slaughtered them, and buried them away in the basement where he slept, where they could still come out and haunt him in the night. Which they did.

They sure fought a lot still, though. About what, Leo couldn't tell. He wondered what these two elder persons possibly had to fight about. They're retired, they own their house outright, they're considerably healthy. They no longer needed to make a fuss about their body parts and what to do with them. They made it; they won the game of life. What's left to bitch over? What's on TV, and what's for dinner, apparently. Whatever—he was an adult now, adults fought, and whether his parents' love was still unified and pure no longer mattered nor affected his potential, like as a man and future lover, or something; maybe, he realized, he has grown out of the phase of being impressionable. Or this was possibly yet another symptom of his *unhumanness*, which he hadn't totally ruled out.

He was more interested in the redemptive aspects of tennis, anyway; how hard work and dedication could get him where he wanted to go, which was away from himself, away from the life he had online. This is what the post-game interview clips of athletes said: "We put in the time. We never gave up. Hard work pays off."

It was Monday, no Tuesday—Wednesday?—when Leo was stopped on his way out, tennis bag in hand, by Gene with his glasses low on his nose, forehead crunched into ripples.

"Heading out?" Gene asked.

Leo adjusted the strap on his bag, pushing it further toward the middle of his back.

"Oh, yeah. Yeah. Going hit some balls," Leo said. "With a client."

Gene sniffed the air.

"Client, huh. I wouldn't last a single day in today's corporate world." He slapped Leo's shoulder. "Lunches, and bottle service, cooking classes and golf outings. You would think half of corporate America was never working at all!"

Leo winced a smile. "The times," he said, ducking out the side door before his dad could answer.

If scouring the Internet all hours of the night for feeling—*something, anything*—is what led to his *unhumanness*, then throwing himself into the world, he figured, would be the cure. What he didn't expect was, he'd have to be *in the world*, with other living, breathing people. People with weird limps, excessive, chaotic body hair, odd smells, and foreheads that looked like knees, knees that looked like foreheads. This was the men's locker room at The Club, an expo center for the bodily repugnant. And he was forced to take it all in, not just click out of it or keep on scrolling. That's what made awfulness online even more repulsive: He always chose the things he looked at. No one pinned his eyelids back and forced his hand. Algorithms are mirrors, not portals; the end result of what you view online is you.

When entering, he had been assaulted by a waft of Ax Body Spray so dense, it lifted him up by his sinuses and carried him over to a bench in front of an empty locker, where he spent several minutes scratching at the back of his throat with his tongue. Most of the men in the locker room were over the age of sixty and were nude, their skin sheening like blocks of cheese. The looseness of their bodies seemed to move independently from their bony core. It all seemed too much to bear for Leo. Too much movement, too much skin, too much *life*. But this is where the man he'd met online said to meet, and so he waited, staring at the head of his cheap racket.

###

He was accustomed to meeting strange men online—crypto gamblers with six teeth in the UK, Russian streamers pounding vodka and abusing themselves with hand tools for donations, Furry boys doing tricks, Canadian Dommes reading tarot cards. But the men he met through the tennis partner finder app PlayOn have been, by far, the strangest; the app uses dating app technology to locate and match you up with tennis players in your area. Some of these men, the Bills and Bobs of the world, all shared an intensity, a more honest self trapped beneath their politeness, that emerged in benign violence, especially when playing sports; they threw their rackets, kicked balls, yelled expletives. Leo saw these symptoms as onset, that eventually he'd see them on the news for some real violence. Other men he had met on the app were bland, so normal, they had to be the opposite, so clean-cut and face-less, they had to be maniacs; and that made them just sad. There was nothing interesting about any of them. They were like cardboard cutouts of men. But these men, he questioned whether, like him, they had some stark contrast between who they were in the world and who they were online. Maybe, he wondered, if he mistook their blandness for what really was a type of Zen; that the truly balanced never showed at the seams. Perhaps they shared his *unhumanness*, walking blankly through life, never leaving a stain.

Rafaelo was a Bolivian immigrant with a long, patchy beard, a round belly, and two large, thick plastic knee braces. When he hit the ball, he let out a big "ooh-ah." Leo could tell from his clumsy heaviness on court, that the man suffered, struggled to be effortless and at ease in anything. His wife probably hated him. Leo wanted to; but he felt nothing. Exchanging forehands with this man was not even considered tennis, it was watching a mouse pointer move back and forth on a screen.

He wondered if maybe a drug or treatment was the cure to his *unhumanness*, not tennis. Maybe if he just found the right doctor online, this doctor could give him an exact concoction of milligrams of various kinds of pills that would make him feel things again. Unless it was something that needed to be removed. So, a surgeon then. A surgeon could cut out his *unhumanness*. Wherever it was lodged, he didn't know. His throat? The fifth chakra, maybe. He no longer had a voice, nothing with authority. Just a series of automated tones to indicate things like understanding, thirst, or hunger, yes or no. He scrolled in silence; the only sound was clicking. Maybe the *unhumanness* was deep in the caverns of his intestines, unable to keep down most foods, suffering from waves of acid rising and falling from his pit up to the back of his tongue. Or, perhaps, it was blemish in his heart area, just a cancerous spot, growing by the minute. That's where he felt a stir of anything, these days, whenever he did feel things. A cold silver pang of his heartbeat. Sometimes it grew to marathon levels, in the dim emptiness in front of his computer screen, breath escaping him, arms detaching themselves from his torso, his head filled with the buzz of helium hovering somewhere above him. This feeling, like a death, was not the opposite of his *unhuman* symptoms; it was the epitome, the climax, a transitioning away from feeling itself.

"Eleven letter word for spilled milk?" Barb called out, from the table. "Theme: Pardon my French." It was mid-morning, Leo sat with his parents in the sunroom tilting his mug, watching the little bit of coffee he had left climb up the side inner wall. Shadow split the table.

"Frappuccinooooo," Gene said, from behind his paper.

"Huh?" Said Barb. "Milk, not coffee."

"So, this is today?" Leo said. "This is what's happening."

"Cow tipping?" Gene said.

"Oh!" Barb said, raising her iPad

Leo felt a small implosion near the center of his chest as his mom leaned over tablet, counting out the spaces.

"Ah, close. Only ten letters," Barb said. "And not French. Good guess though."

"I'm thinking about killing myself," said Leo.

"No," Barb said. "Spilling."

"More clients today, Lee?" Gene said, lowering the right-side flap of the paper.

"Oh, yes." Leo said. "Fully booked this afternoon."

"Lait to waste!" Barb yelled.

Leo raised a single eyebrow, then sat back, looking for something, with a strong intent, in the black liquid swashing in his cup.

"They call it touch screen, but you can't feel anything you're doing."
— Simon Kako, founder of UNPLUG (Us Never Planning to Live Under Gigs)

Leo had rolled his eyes at this ad, three in the morning, on Reddit.

Out of desperation, he agreed to play again with Rafaelo. They exchanged pleasantries as they warmed up, both standing about five feet from the net, ten feet from each other, hitting low, soft lobs back and forth. With every few hits, it was like something urgent occurred to Rafaelo, like a thought that insisted to be freed.

"Nice day out, eh."

"So, my wife decided she wants a puppy."

"Have you ever heard of this Gouda cheese?"

Meanwhile, Leo's grip on the racket handle grew more tense, his eyes, heavier. Maybe, he wondered, there was something about physical exercise that released thoughts from their tiny cages, that when getting the blood pumping, the brain needed more energy elsewhere, and couldn't handle hanging on to these petty flashes of words for too long. So, that's what all of the fitness gurus on Instagram were going on about, as if it were a kind of high. Maybe everyone online was doing their best to eradicate thought. The gym rats were lifting it away; the track athletes were running away from it; the dance trends turned it into rote moves; pop songs replaced it entirely; journalists spun it into news, the comics into jokes; maybe his *unhumanness* was a thought problem: an excess of it.

"I just found this great deal to do my taxes online."

"There's a Greek deli over on Martin, you should try it."

They both agreed to move back, exchanging slow, loopy balls until Rafaelo asked if they wanted to play some games, maybe a set. Leo didn't feel ready for a set; he'd never played more than a single game, which he lost in straight points––double fault, double fault, double fault, double fault. But he said sure. Anything to shut him up. He also thought, that maybe if he was in the middle of a game, he'd lose himself in it. He would just play. He would free himself of thought one hit at a time. But as they started playing, exchanging rallies, Leo began to lose the sense of his own body on the court. Without realizing it, he'd be on one knee near the net, or far out past the baseline, with no recollection how he got there or what kind of shot he'd hit. When trying to think back over a point, he realized he was only thinking thoughts, narrating the game to himself. *Turn the wrist over. Get there. Whip the shoulder. Come on.* In a moment, while Rafaelo caught his breath before serving, Leo looked up to the rafters to see dust particles hovering around the rim of the industrial lights and was flooded by thoughts: physicality didn't remove thoughts, it enhanced them, which was no different than being online. It felt like being a brain without a body. Whether you're active or not, the brain was behind the wheel, while the body was simply the car, which was the first thing to fade away on long drives and high speeds. Rafealo called out, forty–love, then game, set, match, before Leo even saw the ball.

Leo kept awaking from the same breath-stealing night terror that he was stuck in a burning room with his parents and no matter how much he yelled and showed them various exits, such as a fire escape or a cold door to a smokeless hallway, they just stood there holding each other's hands and slow dancing, like they couldn't hear him, or wouldn't hear him. The thing was, he couldn't leave without them, so he tried to get their attention by lighting himself on fire, like a fake fire because it didn't hurt, but his parents didn't notice and just kept dancing until they, too, were burning but like, actually burning, and Leo could only watch from a veil of painless flames as they turned to ash before him.

Rafaelo asked to play a fourth time, so Leo took it as a chance to try to disprove his last findings; he would be conscious on court, aware of the motions of his body. That was what always made him a poor athlete growing up—the coaches called it a "bad head," his inability to just act, physically, without thinking. But after their warm-up and moving back to the baselines to get up to full speed, Leo felt his body fading away from him again. He felt like a floating head out there chasing down the ball. They started playing a game. Rafaelo's serve. The ball was on its way.

When Leo was deep in a full-out doom scroll, hours into a single thread or feed, endless images of vile—news blogs; nefarious corporations with overseas money laundering; drug cartels; crooked police unions; pedophile rings; sex trafficking; gang shootings; poison attempts; riots; looting; mass protests; audio tapes of drug trials from institutions; stories of the insane, people muttering nonsense to themselves in dim lit hallways; kids blasted on drugs and killing their parents; homeless men and women doing ungodly things for money, for revenge, for fun, for chaos; people leaping to their deaths, in front of trains, off buildings, and bridges; murders; throat cutting in the middle of the desert day. When all of this flashed before him, he felt nothing, not a single thing, especially not his hand guiding the cursor, a gentle swipe of the fingers along his mouse. He was a pair of eyes, set to watch.

On the court, it felt the same. He watched as the ball came and went, Rafaelo went back and forth, his arms and racket swung out in front him, his feet shuffling beneath him; but he was never in control, even mid-rally, when Rafaelo returned a low, slow one back, and he darted forward to return, and a band snapped and shot upward from his ankle. He fell to the floor, as warmth and pain rushed toward the spot, and he was struck with the intense crash of feeling. Everything thing around him fell away; it was just his body pulsating.

In the hospital, Leo felt the weak twitchiness of an injured tendon trying to move. It was his Achilles. The foot showed no signs, his toes were idle in a plastic kind of way. A doctor came in, asked him about the pain, and Leo found himself explaining a microwavable bean bag his mom uses for migraines. He rolled over and the doctor squeezed his right calf and his foot twitched. She then squeezed his left calf, and the foot didn't move.

"It's a full tear," she said, "you'll need surgery."

In the bed next to him, on the other side of a thin curtain, he heard a kid ask his mom what the point is of having tonsils in our bodies if we don't need them, that it seems silly and pointless. The mom agreed. Leo waited for her to say something smart and mom-like, something like, "Sometimes things need to be taken away for us to be better." But she didn't say anything, she just chewed on ice chips. Because what could she say that wasn't a lie. He reached for his phone, the magnetic pull of the world within reach to push away thoughts of not walking for a while. But when he lifted his phone, his arm stiffened, then he quickly dropped it, pushing the phone away. He laid back, shut his eyes. All he wanted now was to be left alone with the intensity and heaviness of his body, and its unwavering instinct to heal.

Corporate Son

From over the wall of my cubicle, I hear my boss say to Jerry that from now on all of the duties and responsibilities of a supervisor are his, congratulations. Wow, I think. Jerry? Really? The guy who eats from the seven-layer dip in the break room with his hands? The guy who parks in two spots so no one will come near scratching his very very nice expensive, in his words, "pussy magnet?" The guy whose existence rips at every thread of the fabric of my own morality, my compassion, my sanity? Also, my cube neighbor?

I go outside for a smoke; I don't even smoke. The woman from whom I borrow a cigarette laughs to herself when I light the wrong end, then hands me another. I'm not an idiot, I say. I tell her I know how to smoke; it's just I'm distracted. She says, aren't we all. I don't know her name, but I know she works in Customer Service, so she has the propensity to be polite, to serve, when dealing with some milquetoast who wants something from her. I tell her, you know, this is nice, I think I can get used to it, the smoking, the inhale, the exhale, the time away from the desk. She says, you know what I enjoy about smoking? The Quiet. Those poor customers, I think.

Back inside, I go into the cafeteria and get in line to order a big Meatball Parm sub. That's it, I think. This is what will make me feel better—lava of mozzarella cheese rolling off meatball mountains, all nestled between a cove of white Italian bread like a warm hug from Mom. Maybe I need a warm hug from Mom—but she's gone, so then who? The Indian gentleman from IT standing in front of me in line? I imagine holding him from behind, booking a reservation for one at a table at Le Bistrot Du Human Resources. Maybe Marcia, the HR director, would then hug me, say, "Nico, my corporate son. Things have been rough. Yes. Come here. It's okay. Sh. Sh. Sh."

I'm at the register when I realize I can't pay for the sub, not even a single meatball, so I tell Lucia I'm sorry for the mix-up, and she just smiles, says, "Nico, my hero," with her eyes and "Es no problem," with her mouth, because I know that I just fed her, because I know that the food handlers save the unwanted food for themselves, because I know that my lack of funds just fed her family; I make this mistake daily.

On my way to my cubicle, Jerry pops up out of his chair and says, "Big guy, we're doing drinks and apps tonight at Boylan's. Celebrating me, have you heard?" I tell him I haven't and think that the only thing I hate more than him calling me 'Big Guy' is Boylan's, a dim lit bar with Mobster memorabilia all over the walls. He says, "I'm now your supervisor. You're coming out with us tonight. That's an order."

"Oh boy," I say. "Wow, congrats, Jer Bear. I'll be there, yeah."

"Or you're fired," he says, then slaps my shoulder.

He laughs and I die inside, trying to think kind thoughts about Jerry, like how once he too was a small boy in a world so vast and wondrous, nothing short of magic was possible. I hope it still is as I fall into my rolling desk chair.

Lunch time. I pull out the Tupperware bowl of chili I prepared last night and realize its green lid. I'm a dunce— red lids, my food; green lids, Fin's, my labradoodle, my little prince. I open the lid and yup, there's his dog food, some Purina Beef & Chicken Medley. Hope he likes my chili, I think. I'll ask him when I get home. My stomach makes a sound like my landlord, belching and yelling upwards at my floor. It seems I have no choice here. I dig in my white plastic fork and lift out nothing that looks like beef, or chicken, or medley. Its taste is chalky, and yet, somehow, gooey. I note, cook Fin real food, my prince. Just as I dig for a second bite, Jerry pops up again above my wall.

"What in Trump's nation is that smell? That you, B.G.?"

I feel the chow bleeding through my teeth as I clench a smile.

"Christ, Nico, eat that sock-smelling chili in the breakroom, will you?"

I say sure, and picture Jerry being rocked to sleep by his daddy.

Eating alone at the wobbly table in the breakroom, I count each one of the ways in which I hate Jerry and forgive him for every single one. His perfect hair, forgiven; his sculpted chest, forgiven; his verbal abuse of women in the office, Agh, forgiven; his nice shoes, forgiven; his loud electronic music that overflows from his headphones, forgiven; his awful opinion on most things, forgiven; his inappropriate humor, forgiven; his deviancy on the Internet, his gym obsession, his self-obsessed arrogance, his narcissism, his pseudo-intellectual podcasts, his cheating on his wife with my ex-wife, forgiven, forgiven, forgiven, forgiven, forgiven, forgiven. It's the only way that my online therapist says I will get rid of the rage within my heart. Like cholesterol? I asked her, jokingly via Skype.

75

"Rage is much worse," she said. Now that I have forgiven Jerry for the day, I can eat my lunch—a Tupperware bowl of dog food.

Three o'clock, a calendar request comes in from Darnell, my boss's boss, and it says I've been invited to a four o'clock meeting with him, Sheeba Walts, Yung Mei, and Timothy Gibbs. Wow, I think. All big wigs. Big Kahunas. Head honchos. Yung Mei drives a Maserati. I start to sweat, thinking maybe it's my time; that maybe Jerry got the low-level promotion; that all my work has been recognized. I imagine a fist-bump from Darnell on the way into conference room Q-647, Sheeba standing there holding a plaque that says "#1 C.E.O" on it, Gibbs dropping down to his knees and kissing my Cole Haan's, Yung Mei handing me the keys to a new ride. "Why what's all this?" I say. "For you," they say, in unison like a choir, "Our new C.E.O." I can feel my cheeks rising at the revelry, then Jerry sends me a link to a man in a bear costume getting his penis stuck in a honeycomb. I think about four-year-old Jerry's toes in wet sand at the shore. "LOL, Jer." I type back. "You kill me." Please do, I think. Then I think, bad thought, forgiven.

Before I go to the meeting I stop at the restroom and find Roland, the janitor, on his hands and knees picking up tissue paper, paper seat covers, and candy wrappers from the floor around the toilet bowl. "Aw, Geez, Rolls," I say. "You all right?" He slithers through the bottom of the stall, then comes out through the door that was locked. "Just another day in paradise," he says, tinkering with one of the knobs on the plastic box he carries on his hip. Roland is a former nuclear engineer who once helped develop a healthy way to power turbines; he's a certifiable genius. Worked all over the world. Except folks in

Russia didn't like taking their orders from a black man, so he ended up back here in New Jersey working for a chemical plant. Two years later he suffered something called "The Widow Maker" and could no longer function as a nuclear engineer or survive without carrying this box on his hip that controls his oxygen and blood levels. He calls it his "Speaker Box," and says he loves the one tune it plays: life. So, after all that he's here cleaning toilets at Americorp. And you would never know it, his history, unless you ask, like I did. He told me that not many people do, ask, that actually, he feels invisible in this office; the irony of a nuclear physicist reduced down to feeling like a particle isn't lost on him, he says. So, whenever I run into Roland, I make sure he feels appreciated. After I pee, I tell him thank you for his hard work and that if I get this promotion, he is drinking nothing but the finest wines the French have to offer.

He says, "Boy, your breath stanks. Like my dogs."

I tell him about my lunch, and we laugh. He calls me a good kid. I want to hug him, but he's holding a mop handle. He hands me a breath mint from the front pocket of his jumpsuit.

In Q-647, my stomach hardens and slowly rises; I'm afraid I might throw up all over the conference table. It could be the dog food, or what Yung Mei just told me. She says I'm fired. Canned. Terminated effective immediately. Timothy Gibbs never looks up from his cellphone. I ask, "How is this possible?"

"Turns out we did some auditing," Sheeba Watts says. "And, Mr. Restrepa, it looks as though you've been deliberately ordering food and not paying for it. Just leaving it to be taken home by the food service employees."

My leg shakes. I ask, "And this is a, uh, terminable offense? Forgetfulness? Being penniless?"

Nick Farriella

"No, Mr. Restrapa, it's more than that. It's theft. You're a thief. You exchanged your forgetfulness for a meal ticket and cashed that in to feed our employees!"

Gibbs raises one eyebrow, looks skyward, then nods.

"A debt of 1,500 meatball subs! Excuse me, $15,000!"

"But," I say.

"And we also found out that you were giving company pens to Roland Jefferies, a contractor of all people. And feeding the birds in the parking lot with company-bought bagel bites. And purposely giving Maria your individually prescribed seat cushion with your name on it—"

"She has a bad back!" I protest.

"Enough," Mei says. "It's settled."

"Security will escort you out now," Sheeba says.

Gibbs, still looking into his phone, kicks out an empty box towards me from underneath the table. I envision the three of them as newborn triplets, glossy and shimmering in the clean light of a hospital's Pediatric Intensive Care Unit, their parents lightly tapping on the window from the hall.

I go to my desk and pack my things—my framed picture of Fin, my faux succulent plant, my unwashed bowl of dried crusty oatmeal, my Roget's II Thesaurus, my inscribed journal that says, "N" on it. My corporate life packed into a small cardboard box. As I start to feel as if I were fading away, Jerry's head pops up.

"Heard you got the boot, Big Guy. I didn't know you were such a badass."

"I don't feel like one," I say.

I want to tell him that I feel so low, I might not make it home tonight; that I might as well step in front of a train at Dunellen Station. Might as well drink bleach. Might as well eat a bunch of pills, like Mom. Rest her soul. But I think of Fin going hungry. I think of Roland and his speaker box.

78

I think of Jerry, and that if I'm not around to forgive him every single day then no one else will; Jerry will be damned without me, and I feel even worse for thinking that.

"Hey, hey, are you crying?" He asks.

I tell him it's just dust in the air, that he knows about the air quality in this place.

"Well, you should still come tonight for happy hour. Gonna be the tits."

"Yeah, all right," I say. "I'll see you there."

Beneath a large framed photo of Ray Liotta and Robert DeNiro, Jerry hands me my seventh beer with the foam spilling onto the floor. Boylan's is busy; there's a crowd around the bar, most of the people are from Americorp. An 80s rock song plays over the speakers.

"See," Jerry says, glancing at the row of women near the bar. "The tits."

I don't have it in me to follow my online therapist's orders. I cannot picture my rage as a puppy with a big bark; instead, I feel like a pit bull. All the years of despair, as feeling split in two—an innocent self, born into this world and the spirit of that self, broken by the same world it was born into—feel as if they are adding up inside me. As Jerry stands beside me ogling over the women at the bar, I am overwhelmed by grief. I can't picture Jerry as someone's child, I can't picture him innocent or naive. I'm too low to empathize. His grin, my mother's death, my loneliness, me getting fired, my divorce are all igniting something deep within me, a boiling hot liquid slowly rising from my gut. I see Sheeba Walts, Yung Mei, and Timothy Gibbs clinking champagne glasses on a yacht. I see Jerry in the office getting paraded around. I see him and Celeste in bed, him biting her neck, her moaning his name. I see his cock in her mouth.

"Jerry," I say. "Fuck off."

"Come again, fat boy?" He says.

"I said, 'fuck off,' man."

Jerry rears back and punches me in the teeth; it feels incredible. My head jerks back, smashing into the glass of the *Goodfellas* portrait. Again, my mind says. More. I throw a lofty punch, missing on purpose. Jerry's other fist connects with my stomach. I fall to the floor. Yes, I think. This is what I deserve. As he kneels over me, I call him a piece of shit and a motherfucker. His fists collide with both of my cheeks, one then the other. I spit blood out and let it drip onto my chin. This is what I need.

Now he is being held back by some guys. I stand and swipe at my mouth with my sleeve then charge at the three of them. We crash onto the pool table, all four of us, their weight and my near four-hundred pounds, and roll over the other side onto the floor. I'm yelling at Jerry to hit me more. Blood spews with my words. He calls me crazy then strikes me in the nose. I fall backwards in a hazy bliss; Jerry is my God. I roll onto my stomach and watch from the floor as he and the other guys he's directed go around the other side of the pool table, then lift it, flipping it onto my back. Things go dark.

My eyes snap open to see his Chukka Boots walking away towards the bar. You're not done yet, I think. I need this. Then I stand and start to walk. With the pool table on my back, I imagine that I am carrying the Customer Service Smoker, and the Indian man from line, and Marcia, and Lucia, and Roland, and Maria, and Darnell, and Sheeba Walts, and Yung Mei, and Timothy Gibbs, and Jerry, and Celeste, and my dead mother, and Fin, and every single sufferer on this planet; and with each quivering step they are all saved; that by the time I reach the exit sign, they will be in a better place; that it will be because of me and my penance, and my overwhelming amount of love for them all; that everything I've done will be remembered.

Rules for Escaping

T his is what it takes sometimes. Deep in the abounding brick and mortar towers of Jersey City, an architect from Perk Datt Fowle & Bell Architects Inc. wakes in a room of his own design. The room is on the ninth floor and has no curtains and gets an obscene amount of sunlight. Some days, when the sky has less smog, the window fills with a blue hue reflecting off the river that gives one the feeling they are living underwater. The studio apartment is 10' x 10' and features various gadgets and obstacles that the architect must go through to be let out of the room once the special deadbolt lock is automatically turned over at eleven o'clock each night. His colleagues at the firm call him Memo. This lock, a custom-made electric strike lock, is wired through the wall up to a 240V power supply box that is wired to a six-digit precision digital clock that hangs over the bed in which he is awaking to the grotesque sun. The clock reads 01:00:00.

Next to the twin-size bed is a leather desk chair set in front of an open shelf TV stand crafted of wood and metal support beams with a 36-Inch flat screen TV on top and a basic Sony VCR resting on one of the lower two smoked glass shelves. The walls are painted in Colony Buff. Sometimes when waking, Memo imagines sticking a fork into the tape slot of the VCR and pressing the power button, which is why there are no metal utensils in the studio. Beside the leather desk chair is a TL-15 burglary rated safe, which could withstand sledgehammers, power saws, carbide disc cutters, drills, etc., which cannot be found in the studio either, for obvious reasons; the safe is 1.8 Cu. Ft. and features a custom 8-user electronic lock with a digital keypad. Resting on top of the safe is an envelope labeled "Clue 1" which when he opens it, reveals a notecard written in sharpie that says, "Ling's Birthday."

Also wired to the 240V power box in the wall is a PRO-680DN Box Security Camera that hangs in the corner of the studio and has a 6-50mm motorized lens with 10x optical zoom. The power box itself is wired to a 6" x 6" monocrystalline solar panel which is anchored at the bottom of the windowsill getting bathed in constant sunlight. There are days when Memo's thoughts are aggressively manic, where despite being medicated on 200 mg of Thorazine and 75 mg of Xanax per day, it still takes some deep, heavy breathing techniques in a bathroom stall at the office that overlooks Bryant Park to ensure he doesn't act on them. The digital clock, custom-made electric strike lock, and box security camera all don't turn on with the first glimpse of sun on the solar panel in the way Memo had hoped when he designed it. It takes roughly four minutes of sun (almost twice that on cloudy days) for the charge from the solar panel to ignite the power box which then locks the door, turns on the camera and the digital clock that starts running down from 01:00:00. At that time a buzzer sounds, which one could consider as a type of alarm clock, go figure.

Sometimes the "8" button on the safe's digital keypad gets stuck, so as he goes to enter 090489, it registers as 090488, which on some days is just about enough to get Memo to spiral into a pool of negative thinking so dark and so thick, he could stay stuck there floating for hours. Today, he takes his time entering the digits, ensuring each button is pressed in and released without error; he opens the safe on the first try. The precision digital clock on the wall reads 00:56:41.

Outside, the sky looks like a crystal glass dome. About twelve pigeons rest on the stucco ledge of the building's roof across the street; every few minutes or so they take off in unison and swoop down in a great big wave that resembles the symbol for infinity and return to their same perch. It seems insane, yet beautiful. Once, when Memo was ~11 years old, he found his father's handgun folded up in a dirty rag in a drawer out in the tool shed; he put it in his mouth and imagined pulling the trigger but didn't and the metallic taste lasted on his tongue until dinner. On the sidewalk, a man sells shaved ice from a cart he wheels from a harness strapped over the back of his shoulders like a donkey. It's 7:04 a.m.; the temperature is already at eighty-six degrees.

Inside the safe is a digital alarm clock with a Post-It note taped to the top that says, "Press start to have some space." Memo sits in the lotus position then presses start, closing his eyes as the numbers count down from 00:15:00. He does this daily. Car horns blare in from the street. He feels the weight of his body on the floor, hears the studs in the wall creaking, as if the space is breathing along with him. He feels his thoughts zoom by; some are heavy and sharp and sting a little as they pass. He feels his heart-rate increase, feels his veins pulsing in his arms. His mind wanders. He's in the office, getting scolded for messing up on some prints of a shopping mall. He's in his old bedroom, Ling is there, she's upset, saying it's not that she doesn't love him, it's that it's hard and realer and scarier than she could have ever imagined and that she just about can't take it anymore. He's walking in an empty field on the side of the highway where his car is left in the shoulder and the wind is picking up. He's a child, laughing at pouring salt on a slug. He's over the sink with a knife. He's hanging in the closet by a belt. "Thinking," Memo thinks, and he's back in the room, feeling his weight on the floor, the pressure between his palms and kneecaps. He takes a deep inhale, nestles his focus right up against his breath. The alarm goes off.

The precision digital clock on the wall reads 00:41:12. The bustle from the street grows to a persistent dull buzz. In the distance, a helicopter looms over Lower Manhattan. The smell of freshly made empanadas fills the slot of the cracked open window. Next to the TL-15 burglary rated safe stands a 4-ft. tall potted False Castor or Fatsia Japonica plant. Around the office, Memo is known as "the silent type." He rarely makes an effort to get to know anyone on his team personally and often confuses Theo for Blake and Blake for Thomas. He never says yes to after-work drinks in Midtown. Some of the women around the firm have noted him as "intense." Jetting out from under one of the dark green finger-like leaves of the plant is an envelope labeled "Clue 2" which contains another notecard that says, "Connect yourself with nature," in black sharpie. Memo holds a leathery leaf in his hand. Its veins look like his veins; its tight, smooth skin, feels like his. He holds the leaf up close. The patterns in it look like fingerprints. He looks closer. It looks like braille. He feels around for a message. He's reminded of growth, of cells coming together to form tissue. He is just tissue, not his thoughts, he thinks. Somewhere on the street, dogs are barking.

In the corner of the apartment next to the window is a Yamaha B1 Upright Piano with an open pore dark walnut finish. The precision digital clock on the wall creeps under 00:36:00. Intense, maybe. Although, no complaints have ever been officially filed to HR regarding Memo. Most of the people in the office seem to appreciate his silent charm, which has been taken for granted by some as a type of deep vessel to endlessly shout their grievances into; he's been called a great listener. Resting on the piano is envelope three. Inside is a note card that says, "Create art." His fingers graze the ivory. He plays, not very well, not at all really—just random keys and make-shift chord patterns he learned from YouTube. It sounds garbled and random, chaotic even. To him it feels like Chopin, or Beethoven. His hands move across the line with soft precision; his thoughts trailing away in melodic unison.

After playing, he feels a gentle and light playfulness in his mind. A man can be heard whistling on the street. Standing at the window, Memo sees waves of heat running along the rooftops in the distance, wiggling off right into the performative shimmer of the Hudson river. Memo's mother, Belinda, is deeply Catholic and once told his father George that Memo was born with a darkness in him that no amount of praying or holy water could banish; Memo was seven when he overheard this from the doorway of his bedroom as his parents whispered in the living room. Growing up, he often felt this darkness deep in his stomach, like some sort of worm or parasite lived there, but rather than thinking it was he who was the darkness, it felt that the darkness was the darkness, separate from him, a thing he could rid himself of. Which now, after all the years of doctors and drugs and coping mechanisms, feels true.

The precision digital clock reads 00:22:00. An all-time record, he thinks. But for some reason, the custom-made electric strike lock does not snap open, the finishing buzzer does not go off. Memo walks to the door and turns the handle; it won't budge. He's confused and sits on the ground for a moment to ponder over what he's missed. The pigeons do their infinity loop, but this time don't return to their ledge and fly over Memo's building; one nearly into his curtain-less window. A woman at the bus stop is talking loudly on her cellphone. When he told Dr. Gibbs about his plan to make an apartment designed like one of those Escape Room things, Dr. Gibbs seemed cagey in giving his opinion, but urged caution, because if something in the room went wrong, it could cause Memo to spiral, which would undo much of their progress. On the floor, Memo begins to doubt the room and its purpose, telling himself if he can't remember the final puzzle to get out, then what good is it even going through these motions, day after day. Has he not learned anything? Bill Waltz, the Mid-Level principal/partner at P.D.F. & B.A surely just grabs his coffee, keys, and sportscoat, and walks right out the door. Ling, same thing. This is what makes the final puzzle so important; it's the final test that he can live amongst the normal ones.

Frantic and looking for the final clue, Memo flips over the leather desk chair. Nothing. He rushes over to the potted False Castor and rips it right out of the dirt, throwing stalks of it onto the bed and across the piano. There's shredded leaves and roots and dirt everywhere. He's shaking. The precision digital clock on the wall is dipping under ten minutes. He moves over to the bed and starts tearing at the mattress and pillows with his nails. He pulls up dirt and torn castor leaves and clumps of cotton fill. His fingers are bleeding. He's spiraling; the darkness is creeping up inside him like a wolf coming out of the shadow of the woods. It's there at the line of trees, snarling, showing its teeth. He can't stop tearing the pillows to shreds. He's biting at the thread now; he has become the wolf. He's clawing at his sickness, at all the years spent as this beast. From deep within the pillow, he pulls up a remote with a note taped to the back. "Clue 4," it says.

Memo picks up the leather desk chair from the floor and positions himself in front of the TV. He turns it on. The screen is blue with a message typed in white scrolling across, "Be kind, Rewind," it says. He kneels in front of the open shelf TV stand, presses rewind on the VCR. The tape zooms and makes a hissing sound. The red numbers of the precision digital clock hit 00:04:00. The tape clicks. He presses play, then sits back in the leather desk chair. A shadow splits the room in half.

On screen, he's in the room from an angle above. He is sleeping on the twin-sized bed. He wakes, gets up, opens the safe. Memo watches himself sit in front of the safe with his eyes closed. He fast forwards to him standing at the window, holding the False Castor plant in his hand, through him playing the piano, then him freaking out. He feels ashamed watching this. The man on the screen is someone else; someone far gone, an animal. He winces watching himself gnawing at the pillows with his teeth. He wants it to stop. Before he gets up to take the tape out, Memo on the screen stops and looks up towards the corner of the ceiling; he doesn't remember doing this.

He's watching himself stare directly at him through the camera, through the TV. He sees that he is crying and feels sorry for himself. He wishes he could reach into the screen and hold that man close, tell him that it's okay. The tape ends, the precision digital clock on the wall hits all zeros. A buzzer sounds. He hears the custom-made electric strike lock pop open. The tape ejects, he reads its spine. "Acceptance," it says. He tucks the tape into the back pocket of his jeans. Sirens wail past on the street. He wonders if any of the trains are delayed. It's another day.

Pure Light™

Outside Ann's Tavern, a soggy dive bar on the outskirts of town, Foster meanders through the parking lot, fumbling for the key to his sedan while struggling to hang onto the doggy bag of chicken marsala his Tinder date had barely touched before taking off. It's blistering cold. The wind pushes the bag one way, Foster's coat the other. It's snowing because that's what happens in New Jersey in January, and that's what happens to Foster when he is drunk and distressed: everything just piles up. Struggling to spot his gray Corolla, he spikes the bag and feels subtle relief at the way the Styrofoam tray splits like a skull and the pasta splatters against the pavement. He clicks the panic button of his car remote and waits for its cries for help. His car, shitty thing, is tucked beneath the low hanging branches of a weeping willow, already covered in inches of snow and, with a series of strong gusts, thistles and more snow fall onto the windshield; it's all piling up.

Foster, emotionally speaking, is in a bad place again. He feels himself slip into it, like changing from a suit into hard denim and work boots, a heaviness. It happened right after his date said the words, "This isn't going well, and I think you need some help." What did he say that was so bad? Maybe something about his father? It always goes right back to that with wounded men like him, doesn't it? Oh, no. He remembers now. It was the belt thing. He mentioned, after a few drinks, of course, that when putting his pants on everyday he sees himself tightening the belt around his neck, but then thinks of coffee—like the Camus quote. It was a joke. Or was it? Either way, the look on the poor woman's face. Who says something like that on a date? As she was gathering her things and scurried away toward the door, Foster's thoughts sped up, and up, and up, a tornado of suicidal ideation and self-loathing. The waiter frowned while wrapping up the dinner and handing over the check. Foster paid and moved over to the bar. Four shots of Jack, please. Look at you, he thought, studying his sullen reflection warped by the mirrored Bud Light sign behind the bar. You piece of shit.

Foster is now doing forty in a twenty-five on East Plantation Turnpike, the backroad that cuts through the woods to his apartment. It's out of the way, but he doesn't want to risk a cop seeing him. I swear to drunk, officer, I'm not God. A light snow is falling—a dusting of crystals sticks to the windshield where his worn-out wipers pass over with a honking resistance. The trees lining the thin dark road on both sides are bare and extend over the road, waving in the snowy haze as if it were a crowd anticipating a parade, Foster's drunk parade, a single float hovering its way a few feet at a time through dim cones of dirty light. His thoughts are changing shape, becoming sharper, denser, and taking on the tone of his father's voice. *Failure. What good are you? You should just kill yourself. Kill yourself.*

He's on the verge of doing that thing again, that thing where he closes his eyes while driving.

91

#

PureLight™ is a feeling. It's what shows up on a neurological scan when the patient experiences love or joy, or what one may feel when hitting the open road ten minutes after getting out of work and the temperature is warm and the sun is dipping behind a rocky horizon of mountains and trees are casting this glow, a linear shine cutting through the encroaching darkness with a fine edge; and it is so bright and full, a mental feeling that is almost physical—that is PureLight™.

Lene is writing this at her kitchen table, proposing a draft to present at the East Coast Theoretical Physics Association Conference (The ECT-PAC) tomorrow. It's almost midnight and her two dogs—large black labs Newton and Albert—are circling in front of her glass door, just beneath the key holder their leashes droop from. Just as she hasn't eaten since lunch, the boys haven't gone out.

She looks at them over the frames of her cloudy RayBans and says, "One minute, guys, okay? I'm onto something here." She scribbles more thoughts:

- PureLight™ will cure depression.
- PureLight™ can be bottled and sold.
- Imagine consumers releasing the cloud on-demand. On-the-go.
- Huff-able? Snort-able? Consider testing if PL can be solidified or turned soluble.

Newton is practically smiling with his ears back, as Albert is standing now, paws pressed against the glass door. "Okay, okay," she says, sipping the last sip of her lukewarm coffee before getting up from the table. "We'll go out."

Outside, snow is whipping in swirls off the pine boughs.

Lene lifts the collar of her jacket past her ears. She has forgotten about the weather. Like the concept of it. Always too deep into her work, caught up in thought, that whatever the conditions were when she took the dogs out failed to register in her mind. She did, however, remember the news called for snow, but for Thursday. Fuck, she thinks, is it Thursday? That would mean the conference was yesterday.

Newton and Albert pull her along through drifts. Lene admires their camaraderie from the end of the leash, always sniffing around, tussling with one another, playing fetch, tug of war. She tries to think of a time when she felt as care-free and enthralled as those two; must be, what, two, maybe three, years since she has felt such a thing. Watching them roll in the freshly laid snow, she remembers her sister Sandra, who passed last May. Her feet are cinder blocks in the snow, but the dogs drag her down into the bank where the mailbox post is—just the pole, some punk knocked off the mailbox, which now rests on the brick stoop near the front door. The pole has become the choice bathroom post for the dogs; she dares not remove it.

#

Now, further along the winding Eastern Plantation Turnpike, snow crystals are collecting on his windshield, grouping together, galaxy-like, in subtle bursts against the dark backdrop of night. Foster hears the sharp, raspy tone of his father's voice in his head again, a voice that at times he confuses for his own thoughts. You should just kill yourself, he says, over and over again.

After a quick count—a one, two, three—he takes a breath. Eyes still closed, driving along, he focuses on his breath, and his father's voice fades and makes way for a new collection of sounds: the wind through his cracked window, like a whistle; the low hum of his modest sedan's engine. It goes deeper. Beneath the initial layer of sound, his ears are finding individual melodic symphonies, distant and ever-changing, infinitely apart and together all at once in temporospatial territories; a grasshopper rubbing its legs in the tall grass, a steady drumming in the rubber pounding on asphalt. He lives inside these spaces now, or they are living in him, filling him up.

By now, the third time driving with his eyes closed, he knows he is prone to feel things he hasn't felt in a while with his eyes open. He finds the heightening of the other senses when suppressing one, especially at high speeds, blissful. It's overwhelming and exciting. It's not so much as a thrill, but more of a slight frisson, a shivering of his consciousness.

What attracts him the most about this—besides the bodily sensations igniting into hallucinatory focus—is the feel of the steering wheel in his hands; its gentle pull in one way or the other—there is almost a gravity there between ten and two, or tension like a string he keeps in balance. He knows if he tugs this string in one way or the other, his world will crumble. So, eyes closed on a straight away, he focuses on that balance, leaning harder into the gas pedal.

#

Lene often avoids talking about the cause of Sandra's death and tends to roll over any details with a vague finality: that Sandra was too young to go. Those were the most repeated words in her mind since—too young, too young. She was very young when it happened, twenty-three. More than being just too young, she was younger than Lene, which when Lene considers this, usually in bed, half-asleep, she is consumed with guilt from the thought that it should have been her. They were in the car together. Lene knew Sandra had been drinking, but let her drive anyway, not saying a word, in the world of her head as usual. The last words she said? "I can't believe you hate Talking Heads. There is definitely something wrong with you." Then headlights, a head-on collision like two neutron stars. A cosmic event. Milliseconds of wrong decisions, like letting Sandra drive or putting her own seat belt on without considering Sandra's, swirling around each other to build speed and come together into something universally combustible.

Now, as the snow falls in clumps and Newton and Albert squat near the post, she feels stuck in the thought. It's as if a sadness is now frozen in her, or it's piled up and her feet are buried. She feels the cold wind on her knuckles and wet cheeks; they become numb, as saturated things often eventually do.

She looks away from the dogs and over to the small barn on the side of her house, looming above the low roof of the ranch like an older sibling. Looking at her lab, with its windows covered by newspaper, she remembers she missed the ECT-PAC conference. How could she forget? It's all she's been working toward. But she's been forgetting things, more and more since Sandra. She's been letting daily routines slip away, like showering, brushing her hair, etc. She also forgot her mother's birthday, Mark's first public reading as a published poet. It astonished her how much living the other people in her life can do without her. When did this happen?

This is her fault, of course. Or not—blame is easily pushed around. It could be, as she likes to put it, "its" fault. The universe, that is. As a physicist, the Universe is her God; and no one better to take the brunt of shame or guilt than the creator herself. It's the Universe's fault her sister died, the Universe's fault Mark cheated on her. All the evidence of the Universe's wrongdoing is always all around her, while she tries to find the tools to measure and analyze it.

It was right after Sandra's death when she discovered PureLight™. It was the first pleasant day since the funeral. She remembers being able to hear the birds that day, as if it were her first time hearing them; their chirp was fresh and spritely, defrosting from winter, as if they too were bedridden, bitter, vocally hesitant. In the garage, she was working on trying to replicate the life of a star by cross manipulating sodium atoms with lasers. She rigged an old Whirlpool washing machine as an airtight container. Through accidents, she noticed something surreal about the light when defrosting the atom: the beam had died out when frozen and before emitting once again, a small green halo could be seen; felt, too, she later found, by sticking her head down into the loader of the machine.

Over the next few months, Lene became obsessed with trying to extract the same halo. She spent sometimes fourteen to sixteen hours a day reworking the process, often passing out on the raggedy couch in the corner, and missing meals. She started to call this cloud of green mist PureLight™, because of how it made her feel. Pure. When she would stare at it at first, she would cry hysterically; not for sadness, but because it felt like her body was releasing pain. The feeling became almost orgasmic. Enamored, she would dunk her head into the cloud and let it fill her. Her mind went places far from home, far from earth, to other dimensions where things didn't die. She often saw Sandra in this place, smelled her cucumber melon lotion.

The more Lene spent with her head in the washing machine, the more disappointed she became with reality. Her life, the one outside of PureLight™ paled in complexion to what she experienced with her head in that cloud.

In "reality" her sister was no longer there, Mark was a shell of his former self, distant and impotent. Outside of Purelight™, everything seemed gray. Nothing mattered. She eventually fled the house to live permanently in the garage, until she no longer heard Mark's long showers or the hiss of the coffee machine, no coughs, farts, groans, or alarms of human existence. The house became quiet. More space to work, Lene figured, more time with Sandra.

#

Teetering from center line to shoulder amidst a squall of snow, there is a part of Foster that wants to stay in this meditation forever, this liminal state between being awake and being asleep while in motion. Almost a minute passes since he retreated to darkness—it feels like hours, days even. He is breaking his own record. It is alarming how his car has been able to stay straight at this speed. It's the string, the invisible one between his hands keeping him straight, but now he is becoming too relaxed to notice his right hand becoming heavy. It is time to open his eyes. An alarm clock of panic goes off in his chest. But this time, unlike the last, he is unable to open his eyes, or rather, does not want to.

His sedan veers, slicing towards the shoulder with almost a poignant intention. The tires thump over the heavy snow through the grooves of indented pavement, sending waves of vibrations up to the steering wheel. Such grooves are a warning for unfocused drivers. Foster lets go of any caution he had reserved when first closing his eyes. He is fully one with himself and his vehicle floating through the in-between realm of sleep and reality, and all he feels is nothing, or maybe everything all at once—calm, peace, sadness, acceptance. And like a bunch of sounds jamming together to make one, it blurs together to feel like nothing, not even a breeze. His foot is a cinder block on the gas pedal. With the increase in speed, everything falls away. It's just wind and snow, and his thoughts spiraling. He cries, yells with rage, a release. The louder he screams, the freer he feels. He lets go of the wheel, nothing left to hang onto.

His oblivion is disrupted by the front of his car breaking through some sort of screen of dead weight, a tunnel of thuds. He opens his eyes and in a flash of light and sound and swirling snow, Foster's car slams into a tree. The airbags deploy. A cloud of white smoke creeps out from under the hood.

Foster, dazed, wipes the airbag dust from his eyes and from around his mouth. It tastes salty. He stumbles out of the car, finding his legs work fine, his arms, too; he checks them for cuts and bruises. His head feels light, like a balloon, but he takes it as a good thing because he imagines any head trauma would be painful. A stream of blood slithers down the side of his nose. He feels it running from the bridge of his nose, down into the valley of his cheeks, pooling near his lips, then dripping off the crest of his chin. He lifts his hand to his nose which feels doughy and foreign. No pain, not yet at least. He gets out to investigate.

Leaning against the driver-side door, he hears a series of moans from outside of his swirling thought patterns. He thinks, I'm okay. I'm okay. I'm okay, mostly just to convince himself. For a while his muffled panting, audible to himself from his own mouth through his pressure-filled ears, is the only thing that reminds him he is still conscious. These other moans are different, though; unknown to him, guttural and primal, from something weak and dying. He turns towards the noise and sees its source: a large deer pinned between his car and a tree. Its body is slumped over the hood. Its insides are splayed in textured swirls of red, green, and brown. A panic rises in Foster. Suddenly he feels the heaviness of this situation—which his mind decides is too much to bear and tosses it far away from any point of contact, so far away, that consciously he couldn't touch it if he wanted. This is not real, he thinks. This is not real.

#

Outside, something is changing with Lene. She feels it, standing in the snow looking over at the garage. The conference has passed. What's next? Did Dr. Feckstall call? She doesn't remember the phone ringing. Then again, the phone doesn't ring when it is unplugged. She's sure to lose the grant money, she may even lose the house. The coffee stained and cigarette ash covered envelopes could be the overdue mortgage reminders. Standing over the dogs, she reaches up and tugs on a fray of her natty curls and pulls off a tiny clump of snow. She investigates the crystallized particles, analyzing this frozen bond of atoms. How quickly her life fell apart. She doesn't feel sad about this—no, just a wonderment, like an experiment gone wrong. It was just a minute ago her and Sandra were young girls, sharing books and talking about boys, yet it feels so far away, like it was never there at all.

Albert and Newton are finished doing their business and Lene lets them sniff around the end of the driveway. She isn't sure how long she has been staring at the garage, knowing what lies in there and what awaits her. The snow is starting to yield, and she can see a clearness in the distant sky—a coupling of stars, a shifting satellite, a passing airplane. She is ready to bring the boys inside but when she tugs the leash towards the front door, Newton starts barking, and Albert riles up, too. She turns to see why the ruckus and sees a man with his face covered in blood approaching through the snow.

#

Foster opens his eyes to a bag of Purina Dog Chow next to an old top-loading Whirlpool washing machine with wires veining along its side, being held by duct tape, with a clear dome over the loader. Post-It Notes with inspirational quotes are stuck in color coded clusters along the garage door; newspapers block out the windows. Squinting, he can read a few of the blue notes. They're all science related. *Einstein proposed the theory of relativity in his underwear! Another reads: The eARTh without ART is just eh...but without SCIENCE, it doesn't exist.*

His ears have a low ring in them, and his head feels like it's tied up in a tight knot. There is a familiar air to this setting. It reminds Foster of the garage in the house he grew up in, with its thick clumpy piled geometric area rug, wool woven couch, and the faint hum of old track lighting. For a moment, he considers the possibility this is a dream. He always dreams cryptic scenarios like this: heavy visuals of memories mixed with fears and emotions, always waking up trying to decipher the meaning. With his head slightly cloudy, he starts to believe this is one of those dreams.

He stands, bends to touch his toes, then falls forward rolling onto the floor, laughs. His balance is way off. He is a child again, rolling around on the floor looking for dusty pennies under the couch. For every penny collected, a nickel in return, his father's rules. Where is his father now? He should be in at any moment. After all, the game is probably on soon. Foster figures he will stay still on the floor or inch around like a slug until his father comes in, smelling of bourbon, to pour a little salt on him—you know, give him a good lick for not cleaning up his toys or for existing.

Maybe his mother will follow, calling out, "Dinner's ready." His savior.

Beneath the couch, Foster sees a shining object. It looks like a diamond ring. It blinks, so he reaches for it, slightly lifting the couch with his chubby forearm to get through to it. He grasps it and pulls it in. Instead, it is a human tooth with a silver cap. What are the chances? He is definitely dreaming. Did he will this to fruition? What else can he find? He rises to his feet, stumbles over to the washer, rigged with all sorts of wire and duct tape. He lifts the clear dome lid. A woman calls out.

"You're awake," she says.

Foster turns. This woman is not his mother. She has hair of wild vines the color of barley, wears an oversized sweater drooping down to her knees like a lab coat, and has big glasses with streaks smeared across the lenses. Her intense eyes remind Foster of a painting he once saw of a panther hiding in a bush. This must be someone he has met before. He read somewhere that you will always dream of a face you've seen, even if it's just a face in the crowd.

"No, I'm not," he says. "I'm dreaming."

"And I'm Lene," she says.

Foster smiles, mutters, "Like Renee but with an L."

"Right!" She jitters with excitement then flashes over to sit next Foster on the couch.

"You were in a crash," she says.

"A crash?'

Foster doesn't remember the accident but when Lene mentions it, he feels his head pulse. His therapist, Dr. Frankel, had told him dreams don't have a starting point. "So, if you could remember how you got to a point, you weren't dreaming. Also, time never shows in a dream."

"Is this the time?" Foster asks, reading an LED screen on top the washer. "09261996?"

"No, no," Lene says. "A time, sure, but not the time."

"What is this thing?" Foster asks.

"Just something I'm working on. Come, sit down."

Lene motions toward the couch. She looks anxious. Her mannerisms are robotic and very odd. She sits with her back straight, hands on her thighs, with a bulge in her lip like her tongue is guarding something. While she stares at him, Foster can't stop checking out the washing machine. He considers the possibility this is still a dream.

"I'm so tired," he says. "Have you ever slept so much you wake up feeling like you are still sleeping? Or that you haven't slept at all?"

"I more so don't sleep at all. I'm a scientist." She smiles a jagged, spotty smile, her tongue flipped up over a section of her top row of teeth. Foster sits back down next to her, leans his head onto the backrest of the couch. The track lighting above blinds him so he closes his eyes and asks what kind of scientist she is. As Lene explains her background, he listens to her voice trail in and out of a place he doesn't feel comfortable in—theoretical physics, high energy theory, condensed matter, cosmology.

"So, the washing machine is some sort of experiment?" he asks.

"Sort of, yeah. And it's not a washing machine," she says, then changes the subject. "Do you know what happened to you?"

"I remember being very still, almost like I was floating. Before that I remember leaving Ann's Tavern. It was snowing. I must have pulled over and shut my eyes for a minute and then I woke up here."

"But your sweater—"

Foster looks down into the blood-stained wool of his sweater to see deep swirls of purple and red. He's enamored by the mystery of not remembering bleeding, by having bled without conscience.

"You walked up to my house," she explains. "Bloody

and mumbling something about this not being real."

To this Foster stays silent, remembers being in the road, beside his wrecked car, repeating back the line in his head. *This isn't real. This isn't real.*

"To be frank, sir, well, you look like hell," Lene says.

"You ever been?"

"To hell? No. No. I don't believe in that kind of thing—I do think this is some sort of hell, though."

"So, you're religious? And a scientist?"

"No, silly. But I do believe that archetypes matter. That the word 'hell,' and its meaning is very fitting for the world—this is why science matters. It's our job to figure out how to ascend to heaven."

"And you believe this?"

"I don't believe anything. I hypothesize, test, analyze."

"That I can agree with, believing in nothing."

Foster feels unsettled. He stands again, walks over to the garage door, gawks over the illegible writing, only seeing the name "Sandra" everywhere. His head feels unscrewed, so he returns to the couch beside Lene before anything comes spilling out.

"So," Lene says. "Do you remember what happened to you in the road?"

"I think I may have hit something."

"Do you want to call the cops?"

"No cops," he says. "I'd rather go back on my own."

"Can I get you anything?"

"Can you wake me up?

Lene gives him a blank stare.

"I'm dreaming."

She pinches him in his side. He says, "What you do that for?" Lene laughs uncomfortably. Within her cackle, Foster gets a good look at Lene's missing front tooth. She says she did it because in dreams you can't feel pain, right?

"What happened to your tooth?" Foster asks.

She explains, "One night, about a month after, um, after, um, she passed..."

"Who passed?" Foster asks.

"My sister."

That after her sister passed, Lene went on feeling so terrible about the whole thing that she was in physical pain. Little by little, her body started reflecting her emotional hurt. First, it was something as slight as a twist of an ankle, then a stubbed toe, and a bad burn from the stove, so by the time she got a really bad toothache, she was so fed up with feeling all sorts of pain, she went off into the garage and pulled it out with pliers.

"My husband—at the time—thought I lost my mind, had me put in a hospital for two weeks."

Foster stands, widens his eyes, still unsure if this is happening. What kind of person pulls out their own tooth? He raises his hand to feel his nose; tight, sore, and sensitive.

"I know my fair share of hospitals," Foster says. "Bleach and blistering light."

He tells her that when he was sixteen, his mother died and shortly after that, after the bottomless depth of his grief, he thought it was best to join her, but didn't know how to go about it.

"I didn't remember how I got to the tracks. I just remember following her voice. They kept me in the ER for a week."

"I can still hear my sister's voice—she still talks to me. In there," she says, nodding over to the washing machine. A feeling comes over Foster. It's a disturbance in the lighthearted way the garage felt to him when he first woke up. Now, the garage feels damp and dark; there is a thickness to the air. Foster asks what she's talking about.

"In there, time falls away and pieces itself back together in whatever ways you want. You can be with your mother again. Look." She stands and guides Foster over to the washing machine.

"In here, I'm with Sandra again. It's real. I've discovered something wonderful about the properties of light." She lifts the clear dome and nods to Foster to dip his head into the hole. He does. He hears Lene pressing buttons, turning dials. He waits.

"Another minute," Lene says.

With his head in darkness, Foster thinks of where he wants to go. He closes his eyes and thinks hard. What he wants to see is his father, or maybe not even his father, but some biological throughway, a direct line to a moment, a shift that was the origin of his hurt. Something to explain his grief. Maybe it was something his father did when he was a kid, something unhinged or violent, that tainted his DNA, or maybe his great great grandfather had conjured up something evil, scarring the family. Was trauma a stain in lineage? Poison trickling through a bloodline? That way, if he could just see that moment, where it began, he would know what caused this, and he could say, okay, now I see it, name it, and know how to get over it. How to move on.

"Okay," Lene says, "It's on! You should feel a slight buzz, almost like an electric haze. You may even smell something—for me, it's begonias, Sandra's favorite, but you may smell something that your mom loved. Do you feel anything?"

He doesn't feel or smell anything.

"It's on full blast now! How's it feel?"

Still nothing. Foster lifts himself out of the loader and looks at Lene, who's hiding a giddy smile behind the collar of her cardigan. He says to her that it worked, that he feels much better. Lene nudges him out of the way. He stands back as she lowers her head into the machine then remembers why he was staring at the washer machine earlier. It isn't plugged into anything, and the dials are glued onto its face. Foster finds the couch again, tilts back his head, and closes his eyes to tune out Lene screaming, "Sandra! It's you!" He starts remembering more details about the night: the driving, the snow, him closing his eyes for too long. Did he do that on purpose? Did he fall asleep? That's right, he was closing his eyes while driving again. He starts to feel a deep shame in thinking that he chose to close his eyes for good this time—he wanted to end his life. This goes against what he practiced with Dr. Frankel; he learned forgiveness, compassion for himself. That's why he tried to start dating again, wasn't it? To put himself out there. There's always new things one can do. He slipped up, he drank too much, is all. This isn't real. This isn't real.

Later, they are in the kitchen eating grilled cheese sandwiches. Foster isn't eating much, more so ripping off pieces and tossing them over to Albert and Newton, laughing as their paws slide on the tile. Lene looks thrilled. She reaches over, filling his mug with some coffee.

"You're the first person saved by PureLight™," she says. "This is groundbreaking."

Foster nods and smiles with his cheeks full of bread and cheese. He feels a little guilty for lying to her and telling her that her washing machine cured him of his clinical depression and suicidal ideation. Yet, there's also a part of him that feels slightly better. He can't remember the last time he sat in someone's kitchen, watching dogs, and laughing—actually laughing, too. Maybe tonight is a start—like Dr. Reilly said once, sipping from a mug with a

smiling hiker on it with a caption saying, Life is Good™.
"Depression is something that can always be climbed out
of. It just takes finding the right boots, socks, canteen,
trekking poles, sunscreen, etc. before taking the first step
of the hike."

Foster thinks this is bizarre. It goes against every rational
thought he's ever had. This woman is out of her mind. He
debates calling the cops—not to get back to his car—but to
come take her away. That's what his rationality is telling him,
that this woman needs help; but what he feels is different. He
feels euphoric and present, and Lene is kind of beautiful. He
envies her drive, wants to bottle it up and drink it. Who is
he to ruin this woman's delusion? So, what, he can keep up
with his own delusions as a sane man that pretends to enjoy
his small, meaningless life? But she can't? Maybe how to live
is in the stories we tell ourselves, and surviving is tweaking
the narrative a bit in our own favor. Look at this woman,
he thinks. She's beaming with happiness. It's contagious. He
feels infected. If this sensation is some sort of precursor, or a
hint at a possibility of feeling more of this elation, then maybe something did cure him.

He pours some cream into his coffee, stirs, and then says,
"It's true, Lene. You've done something truly incredible.
You're a genius."

Flaming Hawk

On la noché de las velitas, the night of the candles, my family was setting up a vigil for my dead brother in the shape of a hawk, his favorite bird. We used almost 300 candles, lining them like dominos on the cobblestone sidewalk of the plaza. The entire city took to the streets to make candle vigils of their own. From the sidewalks up to the ledges and windowsills, across store fronts and rooftops, drops of fire in glass and paper lanterns turned Pereira into a scatterplot of light. It was our chance to be born again.

Pistachio shells fall in a ceramic bowl
The ringing is sharp and incessant
One by one
I'm sent back

My mother wept as she knelt down to light each candle, saying Juan would have loved this. My father grimaced, saying something I couldn't make out, as the clinging of shells rang louder in my ear. I saw Juan's face, smirking in front of the glow of the TV, cracking open pistachios with his teeth, spitting the shells into a bowl. He was calling me an asshole. He looked like he did when he was fifteen, messy twines of hair covering his forehead, fat mole on his left cheek. We were identical twins, aside from that mole, the only thing that told us apart and for some reason, made him better looking. I reached out to touch him but found only air. My mind started playing these tricks since he died, following sounds through tunnels into the past, seeing things that weren't there.

"Mijo, you deaf?" My father asked.

The sound drew me away from my family, towards the tents in the corner of the plaza, where the Romanis had set up camp for the holiday season. They were so mystical with their magic and inventions; I was drawn to them after the year I'd had.

The tent was covered in bright-colored medallion printed shawls. I saw smoke bellow from the front slit, and smelled ash and frankincense. Inside was like a shop, so I slouched around with my hands in my pockets, gazing over handmade iron jewelry, wool ponchos, leather belts with patterns burned into the faces. Hammocks hung low from the roof. The ground was covered with metal pots of different sizes. Everything was for sale. I felt dreamlike, not in control of what I could do next.

"If it's answers you want, those are also for sale," a woman said. I didn't see her come in, but she sat on a stool made from an elephant's foot, holding a bowl of pistachio shells. She wore a floral scarf tied around her head, had deep blue circles painted beneath her eyes, and large hoops for earrings. She looked like a pirate, waving me over to the stool next to her.

I paid 40,000 pesos for her to see my future in some cards; I would have paid anything for her to tell me that everything would be okay. That with the changing of seasons, I would start sleeping again and stop seeing my brother whenever I closed my eyes. The worst part about finding Juan was seeing me dead before recognizing it was him. How strange it was mistaking my twin brother for myself, seeing the same long nose and hallowed out cheeks I've been seeing in the mirror all my life, there they were, the flesh drained of color, strung out on the couch. My gut hardened and dropped. The signal shared between us was suddenly gone and, for the first time in my life, I felt unbearably alone.

She rubbed oil on my hands and said to take a deep breath. As I did, she smeared the same oil on the cards as she shuffled them. I coughed, but the musky oil hitting my nose, though harsh, was revitalizing, like smelling salts.

"I see cancer in your future," she said, with a wide smile, pointing to the pack of Derby's in my breast pocket. I said, "I bet you see death in everyone's future."

She laughed, put down the cards then flipped one over.

"This is you," she said.

On the card was a barren fig tree.

"You no longer produce fruit. You are mourning the death of yourself. Let go of your past self, it's dead and gone."

Skeptical, I sat back and smirked, crossing my arms. I removed a cigarette from my pack, lit it, and thought of a few other things I should have spent my money on; Aguardiente, especially. She turned over the next card. It was a panther, stepping out of the woods, its teeth showing, eyes blood red.

"This is what haunts you," the Romani said. "It's at the edge of the forest now, ready to strike."

Good, I thought. In the panther, specifically in the blackness of its glossy fur, I saw the deep centers of Juan's eyes. Maul me, I thought, tear me to shreds. Drain me empty of this grief.

"With the changing of the season, the Virgin Mother allows us to shed any darkness that has clung to us all year. This is done through fire." My mother said, as we looked over the hawk. If I stared long enough into rows of candles, it was as if its feathers were shivering in the wind. So, what, I thought, this vigil was supposed to bring him back? Or now that we took part in this night of showing off skills of sidewalk candle art, Juan dying was supposed to make sense?

La noché de las velitas was Juan's favorite holiday. He used it as an excuse to throw away all the bad shit he had done all year and convince us he'd start the next a different person. It was always the next year he'd get clean, the next year he'd stop stealing. The thing was we always believed him. Like the Romani's cards telling me what's next, we always believed in what was to come, as long as it was better than what had passed. How strange it is when you're told what your future holds, but there's still something holding you back to the past, an inkling that nothing will ever change.

"Make a wish," My mother said.

I closed my eyes and pretended to make one, pretended that wishing for things still mattered. Just then I heard screams at the other side of the plaza. People were chanting or crying, it was hard to tell over the sound of the drums and bells of the band parading down the street. Men in Santa costumes on stilts, women twirling in elegant, flowing dresses; it was like the spirit of Christmas rose from the pavement and crept down the street with the resplendence of a muster of peacocks. Something stirred in me, boiling to the point where I felt restless in my own skin.

"Look, Mateo," my mother said, pointing to the middle of the parade, where a papier-mâché animal, held up on sticks, waved around as if it was creeping through high grass. "Look at the panther."

Beside it, another parader held up a large barren tree made of cardboard and bundles of branches. The panther circled the tree. In its beady red eyes, I saw fire and death. It noticed me. I became too terrified to move. The sound of pistachio shells falling into a bowl grew louder in my ears and I said shut up, shut up. I closed my eyes and saw Juan, this time how I found him. I blinked, and he was there in the parade; the panther, him, and the tree, all standing out and rushing towards me. He was next to me and in front of me; I couldn't get the ringing of the shells out of my ears.

My dad said, "Calm down."

I tried but the panther was in my face now, I could feel its hot breath on my chin. I jolted and swung and kicked.

"Mijo, cuidado! The hawk!" My mother cried.

The panther leapt toward me on my knees in front of the vigil. Just as I cowered back to embrace its bite, the flaming hawk rose off the ground and took flight. My mother screamed. I prayed to God, to Juan, to myself, to I don't know who, to get me out of this. I was tired of walking around as a reflection of my dead brother; I was tired of carrying him around. The hawk screeched and soared above the lights of the plaza before crashing down, where he would surely engulf me and the panther in its fire. I would lay there, burning and burning, bright as a freshly lit wick, shedding my darkness one lick at a time. It was the time of the year to burn the past away.

Binary

It was the beginning of what the Farmer's Almanac was calling a dry summer. When I read that on a rainy February afternoon in J&J's Cafe, I couldn't really comprehend its meaning. It was like reading about how bad smoking is, as you smoke a cigarette.

Four months later, now sitting upon a ridge overlooking an arid lakebed, the term "dry summer" was beginning to make perfect sense to me. Sweating and stoned, my girlfriend Mara and I sat looking out across a massive dust bowl of clay and mud. It was a three hour hike up to the top of the ridgeline, and we had stopped at different vantage points to look out and pass a one-hitter. After three hours, one expected a certain type of pay off, some exchange in currency of visual pleasure for time hiked. Yet, at the end of our footslogging, we were met with a landscape that could only be described as barren. Everything was dead and rotten. The trees were naked and bulldozed over in the mud, awkward in their bent bare state. Even the rocks took refuge away from the pit, jagged and reaching upwards toward the sky, toward an air of hope. In the pit of the lake, there were pointed skeletons of fish fossilized in mud. There was waste scattered around like coral reefs of garbage. There were wrappers, papers, beer bottles and cans, a Taco Bell cup, a few McDonald's bags strewn about. It was as if Corporate America had staked its claim in the litter.

After staring out at the dried lake, a haze of insects hovering above its surface like a thin fog, we began to unpack our bags. We'd brought with us a blanket, a pillow, a canteen of water, a paperback book, and a solitary joint I had rolled on the car's dashboard as we drove in. We made ourselves comfortable and I laid back to light the joint. A strong gust of wind blew over the lake, putting out the flame of my lighter. After three flicks, hidden in the cove of my hands, the joint ignited and another breeze passed through us.

"Do you smell that?" Mara asked. She was lying back with her book resting on her stomach.

Yes, I did smell that. It was the raunchy stench of dead fish; a smell that my senses associated with the Jersey Shore, days spent on docks on the bay, reeling up hook lines of crabbing cages.

"It smells like catastrophe," I said.

Mara laughed and for a second, I forgot the tragedy that lay before us, taking in her smile the way one takes in light. It was nice to sit with her. We had been so busy lately, on some sort of separate tracks of our own individual lives, that to sit down and do nothing from time to time seemed like everything. It was everything. Those minutes, minutes where we were inches apart from each other and I could smell her strawberry shampoo, just sitting and looking out at something sort of tragic, and still being able to laugh about it— that was us. In the future we could probably look back and remember the moment as beautiful. It was not beautiful, though. It was mortifying. It was like the end of the world, and it was starting on a ridge in the heart of New Jersey.

Beside me, Mara lowered her paperback and raised her eyes. She said something about coming here as a child when the lake was full. The glittering reel of the imagined memory showed a sparkling sun-kissed lake and a tiny Mara in a one-piece bathing suit, swimmies on her arms, and learning to swim by leaping fearlessly from an old wooden dock. She asked for the joint and I offered a kiss. I felt sublime.

After two more drags, my mood began to change. I couldn't smoke anymore, and I had the sense that I was becoming paranoid. The all-encompassing feeling of finality radiating off the dried-up lake, as if it was some sort of death sun glowing with bad energy, was seriously killing my high.

"I'm good on this," I said, passing over the joint.

I watched as Mara smoked and stared off into the distance. She inhaled and looked out into the pit, inhaled and looked at the shimmering horizon. I could tell she was deep in thought, contemplating something, or everything. At times I had no idea what she was thinking, whether she was enjoying her time with me or not. It may be that I didn't see enough of her, but the times that we did hang out I was consumed with anxiety, questioning every remark, every expression. Was this good enough? Do you need anything? Are you good? These questions paved over any chance I had at enjoying something.

She bit her lip.

"The hike wasn't too bad getting up here," I said.

"The humidity is high," she said.

"I think we left at a good time."

"I'm hungry. Are you?" She asked.

"I could eat. We should have packed lunch."

Mara rolled her eyes back down to her book. Somehow the implication that I should have packed lunch fell on me. It wasn't enough for me to find the hiking spot, pack the car with our things, and roll the joint (which I bought the weed with my last twenty dollars until payday), but I also had to pack lunch. This was a growing symptom of spending less time together, I surmised. There was an awkwardness between us that was never there before. On top of that, Mara had stopped wanting to do things. It was always, "What do you want to do? What do you want to eat?" It was as if she had gradually become a passenger to our relationship, while I was in the driver's seat hammering down the gas pedal.

After about an hour of silence, Mara reading her book and me stuck in my own head with my thoughts, we hiked back down to the road where her car was parked, a thin, snake-like road that slithered between two bulbous hills. The scenery reminded me of a certain drive in which my father had the radio blasting classic rock, with the windows of his '94 Toyota pickup truck rolled down, amid tall cliffs of mountains and forest with a strip of ceaseless pavement through endless green. I don't remember which road it was exactly, but the one we were on now could certainly have been the same, except the green wasn't as endless as it was in my memories. The forest spread before us seemed finite, bound to run into a highway, a shopping mall, a housing development, or a dried-up lake.

"That was kind of depressing," Mara said, starting her car. The radio sprung on loudly. A song from the 90s played.

"Wasn't music just better then?" I asked.

Mara nodded and turned over the dial. Was it the instruments sounding different, as in maybe they were tuned differently that made it sound better? Or maybe the sound of today's high definition is too clean, and washes away any leftover feeling? My father had once said, when watching The Beatles fumble and yell through a set, "That's the good stuff." Maybe that's what was missing, "The good stuff." I gazed out of the window and watched what was left of the landscape blur past. For a moment, my thoughts fell away with the wind, blowing by aimlessly.

"Are you okay?" Mara asked. "You're quiet."

"I'm not sure."

And I wasn't. I felt a sharp pain in my hip, running down into my groin, around to my lower back, and down my leg. It had started on the hike down to the car and had been throbbing ever since. I thought it could have been a hernia, but after Googling what a hernia was, my symptoms seemed a little off.

"Let's go relax," she said, and flicked the blinker up to get off at the next exit, the exit toward her apartment. The '90s alternative rock on the radio faded, making way for something new and awful.

Mara's apartment was on the second floor of an old brick and mortar building that had once been a large dance studio with high ceilings, but the owner of the pizza parlor beneath had grown tired of all the thuds of nightly dance classes and bought the upstairs, turning it into an apartment. He left the floors and the mirrors and built a loft inside with a steel staircase that led up to it. It was incredibly hip, perfect for Mara. When moving her in, I thought about how much energy flowed through the apartment, that she couldn't deny how much foot traffic was once held in that vicinity daily. After the first month of staying there, I wondered if there was a correlation between the thousands of dancers that passed through Mara's apartment at one time or another and my inability to get any sleep there.

Mara was up in the loft, lying on her stomach on her bed and rolling a joint on the cover of an uninspiring issue of *The New Yorker*. I was on the first floor, looking into the mirrors at an angle so exact I could see copies of myself down the length of them. If I peered down a certain way, it looked as if there was an army of my clones looking back at me. I still felt the sharp pain along the right side of my scrotum and as I looked into the army of me, I started to wonder if all of them felt what I felt, however unlikely. To them I was like some defective copy, which was a feeling I had been immersed in when I had met Mara.

At the time, I held an online editorial internship at a small independent press. Since it was online, my office was wherever I wanted it to be, corners of Starbucks, a bench not too far from the lake that eventually dried up, my mom's living room sofa. I would read PDF files of manuscripts and report back to my editor with any revision suggestions, suggestions that were usually ignored. None of it felt like work at all, but through those endless chains of emails with my editor or with the author I was working with, I felt like someone else—someone better, someone smarter. And when that internship ended, I was never able to regain that persona that I put on through a screen, not even for Mara on our first date. I wondered if a similar situation was occurring in Mara's ballet studio apartment with my face pressed close against a full-length mirror with copies of my better self reflecting back, infinitely looking back at the injured me. After a while, my nose smudged the mirror, and my vision was blurred by the fog of my breath.

"Hey," she called down. "You want some of this?"

I could smell the smoke of the freshly lit joint and declined.

She sauntered down the steel steps, wearing only a red

t-shirt, white cotton underwear, and striped pink and yellow socks. She approached with such a sexy calm that I almost forgot that I was in pain. I left behind the army of me in the mirror to turn and be present. It was a perfect time to be enveloped in Mara's goodness. In times of uncertainty, in times of rich anxiety and worry, there was nothing that cured my ailments more so than her. But, it has been so long since our last time, it was like I was craving her and the subtle drips of seduction like a strong kiss here or playful grab there was not enough to quench my thirst. There, with her strutting toward me, I felt the pain of panic both physically and mentally. It was like I had forgotten how to drink. I limped towards her to be saved.

We kissed and kept kissing. Our bodies pressed against one another in an eager unison. My arms wrapped around her waist and hers around my neck. I traced the slope of her back into the rise of her hips and pulled her into me. We fell back onto the chaise lounge chair. She was astride me, leaning over me. She lifted her t-shirt off above her shoulders and started to rock back and forth slowly. And then, pain.

"What's wrong?" She said, breathing heavily.

"It's my—"

She rolled off me and looked at me with concern. Inadequacy was always a fear in the back of a man's mind, or maybe just mine. Perhaps it's not inadequacy, as in not being good enough, that worry men, but rather the act of performing itself was too much to bear. There's another synonym for pretending, performing, as if I wasn't really trying to make love to my girlfriend, as if I wasn't actually trying to please her, but I was simply acting the role of lover. And as the actor, who had minimal training in both theater and knowing which exact inch of skin to touch, which way to tease and fulfill, and balance giving and taking, letting their primal need subside to hers, I was deeply immersed in stage fright. Some performance. Maybe that's why sex is so hard to portray in movies and in literature: it's not real, it's not in the act. It is only a reproduction, yet another copy of something real and flawed, like mirrors or online personas of something better. The only way to fully experience sex is to be in the act. If only I could tell that to my fifteen-year-old self. But as a twenty-five-year-old man, who was in excruciating pain at the time of performance, the only thing to do was to try to please. As they say, the show must go on—maybe acting and entertaining were one in the same, just not when it came to sex.

After explaining the pain, I immediately started getting mother-like sympathy from her. It was impossible to put into words the feeling of being tended to like some little boy, all while still being turned on, still wanting her and feeling her hands on me, stroking, while she was naked and stunning as ever. How different her hair looked. Maybe it was the light or the way I perceived it through the half-squinted blur of pain, but her hair looked amber, tied up in a messy bun. I wished I could just blurt out how beautiful she looked, but was that not just romantic sap that would certainly kill the mood, if a flaccid pain inducing hand-job hadn't already?

Mara gave up trying to get me off. I writhed in pain. All I felt was an electric shock running its course up and down from hip to testicle. She put on her shirt and helped me off the lounge chair. She mentioned something about going to a hospital. I nodded in agreement with fluttering eyes. She muttered something about insurance. I passed out in her passenger's seat, a pop song on the radio.

#

Sue Grimes was the one with cold scaly hands. They smelled of cigarette smoke and resembled death, much like the cigarette itself. I know the way the tobacco residue gunks in the crevices of your nails, introducing itself as a mustard tipped handshake. Sue Grimes, the Resident Nurse at Oak Moore Emergency Department, looked and smelled the part. She took my vitals in the waiting room. I felt exposed as I watched the mother and teenage boy who sat together watching a rerun of *Law & Order*. Weren't all *Law & Order* episodes reruns? With every episode came a strange Déjà vu, a feeling that one had seen it all before.

Had I seen this waiting room before? It held the usual dense air of sickness, the hum of a floor cleaner or perhaps an air conditioner, or some other machinery that only runs overnight. Hospitals buzz overnight. It was all so familiar. There was the mother and son, and yet I couldn't tell who the patient was. My guess was the son. Did it matter? If that was the case, then the mother was not well, either—stress, worry, or what-have-you consuming her as well. Next to me, Mara seemed stiff, biting the lip of a Styrofoam cup that was filled with ice. Her face showed no indication of her thoughts. I wondered, is empathy contagious?

Then, there was the girl—the young toddler who sat directly in front of me with a tablet hiding her face. I had the strange feeling that she was taking pictures of me or perhaps of Mara and me, especially when Sue Grimes and her cold hands placed some sort of electrical shock pads at two locations on my chest. That seemed pretty photo worthy, or sharable. Because of social media the world was still a place for you to offer things. I had a Facebook account for three months and never posted. I felt invisible. Picture this: the girl looking at me through the tablet, seeing a filtered version of me, while I sat and watched an episode of Law and Order, that I had or hadn't seen, all while cringing at coldness and trying to describe the unknown carving of testicular pain to a woman in scrubs who just smoked a cigarette in the rain. There was a hashtag in there, somewhere. I dozed off trying to find it.

I woke up in a room where a Vietnamese or Filipino nurse introduced me to another Vietnamese or Filipino nurse. The new nurse was short and round and had the type of beauty that was made to be plastered all over social media profiles: shining lip gloss, tattoos, skimpy clothing, and various angles of her breasts. She was wearing a low hanging V-neck scrub top of a different color than the previous nurse, meaning she held a different position within the hospital. I once worked security in a hospital. Green scrubs were for surgeons, maroon for techs, and black for resident nurse. What did Gingerbread Men scrubs mean? Especially in June? I sat in my wheelchair in my ill-fitting gown and listened to the two nurses talk, in what I guessed was Filipino.

The first nurse drifted away and left me with the newer one who introduced herself as Luna, the ultrasound tech. To think that Luna had a different history of studies than the previous nurse, relaxed me a bit. It was as if I kept getting passed around to better hands. At least, that was what I hoped.

Luna directed me to lie down on a table much like the ones I ate lunch on in grammar school, thick high-pressure laminate tabletops with benches made of either particleboard or plywood. The thing that set apart afternoons of chocolate milk cartons and packets of carrots from my current adult self was a cold sheet of wax paper.

"All right, Papa," she said. "Let's get started."

Few sensations ever align with others. Some are so unique they can only be described as moments of a lifetime. Scoring a touchdown or hitting a homerun in the big game. An orgasm. Skydiving. All unique feelings that could only be felt in those situations. Nothing in my life has ever, or possibly will ever, align with the sensation of feeling the ice-cold gel of the ultrasound wand rolling over the cusp of my right testicle in an aggressive manner. It hurt like hell, and it felt erotic; I squirmed in place, feeling the heat of pain and shame.

One would think a certain gentleness would be taught, or even a shred of common sense would be had, that when dealing with that level of sensitivity, some caution or even some reserve was in order. For Luna, who kept steady eye contact on a blue lit screen and blindly ran the gel-covered tool around as if she were an infant trying to jam a cylindrical piece of wood into a triangular hole, tenderness was not an option. What made it worse was the small talk.

"So, you like sports?"

"How about this drought? My cousin Ricky said no corn this year."

Luna's words were sweet, but her hands were cruel. There was constant friction and shuffling at play between my legs. I would cringe and squint, all while trying to think of Mara, who was probably asleep in the waiting room. Is the definition of strength not to act normal in abnormal situations, or is that courage? How does one act normal when sprawled in a way that is tortuous; legs open, manhood exposed to a Filipino woman with large breasts and heavy hands? Even thinking of her didn't help. When I did, I pictured her sitting there in the waiting room watching Law & Order. She felt so far from me, removed from the pain I was experiencing and far from the realization that something was wrong with me, or going wrong with me. It terrified me to realize that I was alone on the examination table, waiting and looking into Luna's eyes for any change, any sign that something showed up on the screen that would suggest what was wrong. And if she found something, that meant something in me was defective, a proverbial finger to point, that something that was not only affecting me, but Mara as well.

Minutes felt like hours. Luna clicked and typed, staring at her blue screen that showed a distorted image of, when zoomed out to a great distance, me. The screen showed a microscopic angle of my flaws in ways that I hoped were not cancerous or terminal, and also in a way that I have never seen before. To be reduced down to a graph, to numbers, seemed wrong and unnatural. I had once read an article about the possibility of having your soul scanned into a computer when you die. Someway, that something, somehow stretches your DNA makeup into binary code, each individualistic character of you being assigned a number. Your likes, dislikes, your flaws, your dreams, your desires, your insecurities, your passions: all translating to numbers on a scale. This made me think of technology as a kind of religion. Lying there, staring at the glow of an orange light overhead, I had visions of Internet-based heavens and hells with ultrasounds being the middle ground between the two. I must have dozed off trying to determine the fate of my soul. Yet, at the end of the examination, when Luna nudged me awake and directed me to clean myself off and throw away the six towels that were used, along with the crisp paper sheet that went soggy from sweat, the feeling that I felt could only be described as soulless.

Leaving the emergency room, filled with anxiety from all the ultrasound's unanswered questions, I saw the girl with the tablet once more. She was sitting on the linoleum tiled floor with her face pressed closely against the glass of a vending machine. She was begging her mother for a candy bar. Her mother was hunched over, still draped in a hospital gown, shivering.

"All right, all right," the woman said, "just don't tell your father."

This innocent exchange of secrecy made me feel a little

better. It invited thoughts of secrets that my dad and I had shared through the years. "You better not let your mother find out," he said when he caught me smoking a cigarette under the awning of our porch. He lit one too. "She'll flip."

I smiled at the girl who was getting what she wanted and held Mara's hand as we walked toward the exit.

Outside, in the humid air of a summer night, I heard a breeze cut through the trees. I heard cars whooshing by as we walked down Easton Avenue towards her car. I smelled burning wood and felt a coldness drift in. It looked as if it was going to rain.

"How you feeling, champ?" Mara asked.

"Like I want a cigarette," I said.

"Three days since you quit, and you're already in the ER. At this pace, soon you'll be over there," she said, cackling, pointing to the cemetery across the street.

We drove off in her Honda Civic with the radio off. High on a cocktail of pain meds, I was drifting in and out of a dream-like state, one where the words she said would blanket me with comfort. There are words when said out loud that cause a physical reaction in the body. For instance, when tracking your heart rate on a smartwatch, a graph appears on the face of the watch that shows the beats per minute, or BPM. Some people distrust the watch's ability to be directly in sync with the heart, but no current lawsuit has been settled. Regardless of the technicalities, it has been proven (by extensive research by Mara and me) that there is a spike in the BPM when certain words are heard.

"I love you," she had said on a bright Sunday morning. We were hung over, slung across the wooden floor of her apartment where hundreds have danced, eating peanut butter from the jar with a spoon.

"Any reaction?" She asked.

125

"Increased by eight beats."

We let a moment pass then tried again.

"I fucking hate you," she said. "Anything?"

"Eleven beats."

"I guess it's true, hate is the stronger emotion."

"Eh. Maybe the increase was from you saying 'fuck' also, and not just hate."

A few minutes passed in silence.

"Let's fuck," she said,

"No change."

She led me up to her loft, where, after twenty-two minutes, we were able to increase my BPM by thirty-three beats. "That has to be some record," I said, gasping beside her, grazing her collarbone with a soft finger. She was trying to catch her breath. She checked her smart watch.

"I'm dead."

Her heart rate monitor had flatlined, and then read an error message.

There in the car, on the way home from the hospital Mara had said words like, "cancer," and "tumor," and "benign." Subtly, I kept checking my heart rate via my smartwatch, constantly checking the watch to look for any change in BPM, but when she said "cancer," and "tumor," and "benign," there was no change. Instead, I joyfully remembered the innocence of our time together. What I would do to go back to that moment on her apartment floor. I was focused on her driving and wondering if we could ever get back there. She leaned over to click on the radio then held my hand. Over a pop song, I misheard Mara say, "Hopefully, it's binary," when I think she meant benign. To hope whatever was slicing at my testicle was binary, a set of numbers punched into my body's system, was to assume that somewhere this was all relevant to something. With her feeling close to me again, I thought maybe it was.

I sat back, feeling like a copy of an illness, as if I was

three-dimensionally printed and placed in a car traveling at thirty-seven miles per hour, or what the LED center console told us was thirty-seven miles per hour. I wondered if we were really traveling that fast at all, I felt so still. The street-lights blurred past in streaks of white. Raindrops spotted my passenger-side window. It was getting harder to stay in the same position, the pain still slicing through me. Mara, hand in mine, was focused on the road, still in the brown hoodie she wore hiking, her hair up in a lovely mess.

"You look beautiful," I said.

"Look," she said. "It's starting to rain."

The Boy
with a Void

Monty was born with something missing. The doctors saw it in an x-ray when he was four. What showed on the scan was a small void, next to the heart, that gave his mother an explanation for his odd behavior; he didn't find much pleasure in anything, he mostly just sat there, silently staring off, or walking around, curious, like he was looking for something. Not knowing what it was, the doctor also said there was a chance it could grow which meant he could die at any second and told his mother to teach him that life was precious and short.

Around the age of eight, when the void had grown double in size, Monty had the idea to try to fill it with something. His dad watched a lot of baseball. Every night he was in front of the TV yelling all sorts of stuff, but mostly cheering, smiling. He seemed happy. Monty hadn't really known what that kind of joy felt like. He figured if baseball could keep his dad happy, maybe it could help him feel that way.

One night, Monty went into his father's old woodshed in the backyard where his dad kept a bucket of baseballs with Monty's name Sharpied on the outside. Monty grabbed one of the balls on the top of the pile and went over to the corner of the shed where his dad wouldn't be able to see the candle-light flicker from the living room. In the orange glow, Monty removed his shirt and tried to control his breathing. Staring at the red laces, he thought about how life was short. Before that night, nothing really made him feel anything. He felt sort of like those laces, woven and stitched so tightly into something bound to unravel. Looking at the smallness of the ball and the shortness of life, Monty felt that the risk might be worth it. He gripped the ball like a fastball and jammed it into his chest. To his surprise, the baseball went right in—he felt no pain, only a warm sensation. Once Monty fit the ball into his void, he let go and slid his hand out. There was no blood or anything. He walked out of the shed not feeling complete, but smiling, for the first time in his young life.

The baseball lasted until Monty was fifteen. It got him through some hard times. Anytime he felt pulled towards his inner emptiness, he would just tap on his chest, knowing the ball was there all along. His dad seemed to enjoy it, too. He loved to watch Monty play; he was actually pretty good! His dad said Monty was going to be a New York Yankee. What his dad didn't know was the ball was rotting inside of him. Monty lost faith in the ball's ability to fill his void when he met Judith Hendricks in sophomore Biology.

Before Judith, Monty hadn't really taken an interest in girls, but she loved all the same comics he did and wore her hair in this funny braided side ponytail that drooped over her left shoulder. She was beautiful and funny and smart and after a while he didn't think much about baseball or anything else but Judith. The ball was dead inside of him. He could feel it. He felt sluggish and disconnected. Hanging out with Judith made him feel a little better, but even that seemed daunting. Monty knew that he had to take the baseball out of himself, to free up some space for Judith, to fully let her into his void.

After a school dance, Monty told Judith about the emptiness inside, that he had tried to fill it with a baseball and that it was dead. She didn't look at him like he was crazy. She said, okay, what do you want to do next?

They went to the basement of her parent's house. She propped him up against a rusty washing machine and he removed his shirt. She started to cry and told him she was scared and didn't know what was happening. Monty told her that life was short and whatever happened was not her fault. She said okay, and he said okay. Monty took a deep breath then jammed his hand into his chest. Judith screamed. He told her that it doesn't hurt. Inside, he felt a mix of sharp thread and goop. He pulled out a fistful of it and opened his hand. In his palm was a clump of black tar with hints of the red laces woven throughout. Judith puked. Monty went upstairs to get her mom, told her Judith had eaten some bad chips. He left and rode his bike home, weeping the entire way.

After a week with nothing in his void, Monty felt awful, like he wanted to die. It felt like the emptiness inside had fully consumed him. His mom took him to the doctors where he said the nothingness had grown so large it was starting to cover Monty's heart. His mom had a look on her face that said she knew this day would come. The doctor prescribed him pills that made his head feel woozy, like he was watching the world from the inside of a fish tank. Later, when Monty told Judith about the growth of the void and that he thought he might kill himself, she said she had an idea.

They went back to her basement and this time she laid him down on her couch. She kissed him and said that even though life was short, he shouldn't be the one to determine how short it was. She told Monty to close his eyes, then removed his shirt. She kissed him hard and he fell into a daze. Before he realized it, Judith had forced her hand into his chest and dropped something into the vacant space inside of him. He felt it clang around; it was something small and metal. When he asked what she put inside, she smiled and said, "my locket."

The days got better. Between the pills and Judith, Monty started to feel whole again. The rest was a trip; from prom, to graduation, anniversary after anniversary, holiday after holiday, birthday after birthday. There were bad days sure, but each bad day was a day closer to a better day; Monty found if he could just make it to those special days, he was able to hitch a ride off the high to carry him along a little further. The years ran away like that. Judith went to college at Rutgers. Monty worked for a demolition company in New Brunswick and lived in her dorm. Their small life was good. Monty felt happy. It seemed her locket was enough, that it was the missing piece. At night, he often stayed awake a little longer than she did, imagining growing old with her, living out the rest of his years with this little piece of Judith inside him.

When they were twenty-four, Monty had gotten Judith pregnant. Six months after leaving the clinic, they were on the stairs inside of her apartment, smoking cigarettes. She said she's been having this dream about a void growing inside of her, too. Judith told him on most nights she dreamt of their baby standing at the foot of their bed gnawing at her toes.

"Everything is different now," she said.

He asked what had changed despite what happened.

"It's just that—every time I look at you, I see what we did."

She then told Monty how sad she's been for the past six months, how she grew distant and cold. Monty noticed, but didn't care. He was blinded by the anxiety that maybe the locket was rotting inside of him, because, after the clinic, he started to feel a change too. The locket felt uncomfortable, as if it was lodging itself in his throat, trying to escape. Monty became self-obsessed, only worrying that his void would come back. She said that it was over.

From the bottom step, he watched as Judith went back upstairs, where she called down to him to follow her. He found her kneeling next to the couch, crying.

"I have an idea," she said.

She told him to lie down. She unbuttoned his shirt then laid a soft hand on his chest. She said that this needs to happen, that it's the only way she can live again. Monty said, okay. She took a deep breath then drove her fist through his skin, crushing through the sternum, into the caverns of dark matter next to his heart. Monty watched as her wrist dug into his chest and felt her small hand moving around inside him. Things squished, and bones cracked. For the first time, Monty felt pain. The locket must have rooted itself to something; she was having trouble pulling it out. Finally, after a quick tug, Judith removed her hand and revealed its contents. Another pile of black tar with blue and red vines cinched around it, the locket and its chain buried deep within. He watched as she failed to insert it into her own chest, then settle for putting it around her neck.

After Judith left, Monty felt more than empty, that even the darkness had depths, and he was suspended in its lowest tier. He spent some time in the hospital. The doctors said the dark matter had fully consumed all of his organs. They guessed he only had a few days to live. Monty asked if he could go for a walk.

In the woods outside of the hospital, Monty came across a section being cleared, mostly broken branches and leaves. He laid beside the mounds of brush and thought of Judith. She was doing well, he saw it on Facebook. She was into hiking and nature now. He was happy her void was only in her dreams. He didn't want anyone to know his condition firsthand. Monty watched dark clouds scroll by and thought about how life was short. He heard Judith's voice telling him to keep trying to find what was missing, that he owed it to himself. He knew the abyss would take him soon. It started to rain. Monty could hear his mother calling his name, but he was too tired to get up. With a last surge of energy, he reached out to grab a bundle of twigs and dirt and dry leaves and stuffed it all into his chest cavity. He still felt half empty. He leaned over for some more branches and grass, packing his void until dirt was coming out of his mouth. Lying back, exchanging final breaths with the trees, he thought of Judith sitting in the lotus position on a rock, her hair in a side braid, and felt full again.

Weight of the Clouds

On the morning of the day she promised to make the five o'clock news, she watches her boy lie in the grass from the window above the kitchen sink where her hand shakes holding the knife under the suds in the greased pan with hard webs of scrambled eggs, tomato skins, and chives scraping against her knuckles as she revels in the fact that she had raised a child who can spend time in his own mind and doesn't need some sort of media to distract him, which seems to be a rarity now—she knows from having met a few of his classmates who all depend on a screen to relate to one another, but not hers, who spends afternoons gazing upward—which now that she thinks about it, adjusting the faucet away from the scolding heat, maybe that's not a good thing at all, that maybe he is—like she was at his age—inclined to ruminate, which she knows is a way of disconnecting, and that maybe one only looks skyward when one feels trapped in one's head, the way you would find the light if stuck in a well; and now there's a sudden fear creeping in that she had not expected, that if she had a sensitive little cloud-watcher already, there is no telling what would happen to the boy if she goes through with what she is about to go through with, knife still in hand, telling herself that there would be no bottom to the depths of despair in which her son would descend to, but then again, maybe not really, maybe it would cause a counteraction where the boy is propelled through life with the stubbornness of his father and achieves great things and looks back at today as the day where it all really happened for him, that if it wasn't for his mother and all that she went through, he wouldn't be who he is, but now that she is saying all this in her mind, the more ridiculous it feels and the more she wants to carry out the plan anyway—if you could call it that, it's really an impulse if anything, like if she could strip away the layers of years of pain, through the piled-on suffering, beneath all this, she swears she would find only a simple urge, like an itch to scratch, one that has been there beneath the skin all along, festering like a cancer cell she had inherited—but there is an innocence in the way the boy's high-top sneaker hangs loose over his knee that is pushing her further away from that space, despite the weight of the knife as a reminder and the pan now overflowing with murky water as the sneaker bobs like a lonely leaf on a single branch, dangling there for plucking, his arms folded behind his wispy head as he squints, making shapes in his mind of the passing clouds, completely entranced by the way in which one can feel like the only motionless thing on earth, despite knowing the truth that it's all in constant chaos, knowing that everything is in flux, on a timeline of growth and decay, so, she wonders, in the time it takes for her to wring out the sponge and set the knife, how one continues to lie still and watch the unfolding without batting an eye, and how is it even possible to lie there knowing that the average cumulus cloud weighs roughly 1.1 million pounds and not cower out of the fear of being crushed, but stare back at in awe, and not look away, not even for a second, how, how, how, h————

Float

The beautiful thing was waiting for her. There, bobbing up and down as her head went down then up. Pitched, smashed, a crown of pink, oil slick belly, a bubble slice of rainbow. She afloat her yellow foam noodle, drifting toward it. Glassy turquoise waves rolling. It was out there. An azure balloon of glitter. Gyoza skin. Light held it. It held it back. A toy. She kicked harder to not let it get away. She was seven and wanted it. Something that beautiful and dazzling had to be hers. The colorful floating plastic bag. Translucent and tinged blue and mauve. A single squint, the sun a smear in her left eye. A woman entered the frame, also transfixed on the beautiful thing, pushing toward it. It became a race. A rushed paddle and a desperate reach. Swallowing salt. Diamond droplets hung above their heads. Near now, face to face with holy pulchritude, she extended her small hand to finally touch it. It held her back. An embrace. Long limbs of death unfolded out from underneath. Electricity thrashed through her. Her opponent retreated. She who would win, would lose. Her love stayed. Flashing pain. A thousand knives, a thousand stabs. Her mother yelled from the shoreline. A current of arms brought her back. They took it from her. A light flickering. The wet sand cold and sharp on her back. It was dead at her side, and still so painfully pretty. Everyone around stared and caught their breath. It was still beautiful, even dead. The Jamaican sky dimmed, then went dark.

#

Night, at the window again, lightly panting. The fire escape makes crosses in the pane. A square dusting of clouds, a few stars. Lyle asleep behind her. Renata holds the thumbnail moon in her eye, steadying her breath. The image of the show still burned into the TV. An uncomfortable bright glow of late-night-early-morning fills the room. In the corner, a centipede waits. Beside it a small spider falls and hangs. A truck gurgles by in the distance. She returns to bed, drawing the sheets halfway. She wants to ask him another question. Renata sinks further into sateen, turns onto her side, presses her finger into his shoulder.

"Babe," she whispers.

"Death is like runner's high," he says, still asleep.

She rolls onto her back. The ceiling turns in light.

The bed glows with warmth. There are bird sounds, a ladder of light on the wall. Lyle's hot breath in her neck. She's on her side, on her phone. He pushes his hardness up against her; she pushes back, angles her neck for a kiss, lets out a soft, "You wanna?" They have sex. Lyle on top of her is security, strength. She doesn't have to do anything except melt, and fill out the shape of him, let his form define her. Part of her gets off on this, her formlessness, his direction. After, he draws little leaves off the branches of her stomach scars and asks if she didn't sleep again. She says no, running her nose up the side of his neck. He squeals the perfect little sound.

"I love how ticklish you are," she says. "It's adorable."

"It hurts."

"But it's so cute."

"It kills me," he says. "Like my entire body constricts all at once."

"But that laugh."

"Must be a pain response."

"I love it."

#

Keep your routines, keep your routines, someone once must have said. Maybe her mother. Keep your routines and crunch your day down to a minute-by-minute basis. It's easier to process this way. But processing is the first thing the sleeplessness takes. One minute you are letting the sharp arrows of the shower's hard water pierce your eye lids, the next you are watching the coffee pour into the basin of the machine before realizing you forgot to set a mug. Breaking down things into moments just makes the broken pieces more pronounced, instead of being lost inside a day. In keeping with her routines, she's finally off to work, after having turned back three streets from home when she realized she was still wearing her slippers.

#

Work is a Float Tank Experience Guide at High Spiritual Spa in the Blue Brook shopping mall over on Rt. 22, next to Smashburger and Pets-landia. Renata is in charge of setting each of the tanks' Pod-mospheres according to her patients' Floating Intentions. She warms the water, puts the selected light filters over the headlights inside the tank, prepares the playlist of relaxing tones and singing bowls; she also is their voice-therapy-guide, where she sits in a booth in front of a switchboard that cues her in to talk to various patients while they float in their pods. At High Spiritual Spa, you can choose between five float experiences: Motherly Womb, Ocean Tranquility, Cloud Bubble, Tropical Raindrop, or Galaxy Gaze. Sometimes, in the booth, Pod 1 will need to be told that they are being nourished by their mother's love, at the exact time the light to Pod 4 dings to remind her to say that they are now rolling across the ever-slick plane of a teak tree leaf. This is what can make the job complicated. If she's not paying attention, as she's been apt to lately, lost in the unthought of insomnia, and tells Pod 5, Galaxy Gaze, that the wading tide of peace is guiding them through a burning amber coral reef, then that's a ding on the flotation experience, for sure, and she can bank on a patient complaint and being spoken to by Micah, the founder of High Spiritual Spa, who's standing at the front desk as she enters, in his braided loafers and ponytail, stretching his arms back in a crocheted hemp vest, letting out a high-pitched, angelic ringing, "Mooorningggg."

She puts her purse on the counter, makes eye contact with Leigha, the floral headbanded receptionist, and sighs deep from within her core.

"You have Moana at nine. Cloud Bubble," Micah says, clicking on the four-foot Himalayan salt crystal in front of the counter. The orange glow highlights a dryness in his beard.

"Riveting."

"And Josie same time. She wants to be in utero."

"That's a new one for her. She's usually a galaxy girl."

"Sign of the times," Micah says. "People are retreating to

the womb in fleets."

She winces a little bit every time he says utero.

#

"You are safe in the warm grotto of your mother's bosom. It is cozy and fluid, and you are safe. Muffled sounds of life engulf you. Can you hear it?"

She presses the soundscape button.

"The tones of those who love you are there. Just on the other side of this vessel."

Inside the pod a red light pulses. The water trembles.

"Do you hear the pulse? It is the sound of your mother's love. Do you hear your pulse? It is the sound of your life. They are one, and you are safe."

#

Leigha slides her a vat of beige glittering ointment. They are sitting behind the receptionist desk, while Micah ran out to get three vegan burgers.

"Mercury wave repellent."

"I'm going to break out."

"Minor to those waves. Woof." Leigha extends back. "They're hitting me hard today."

"Retrograde?"

"Major. Moving at warp speed. Isn't it strange?"

"Maybe that's why I'm not sleeping."

"How they call it an optical illusion. Is that an oxymoron?"

"No, it's an actual physical optical illusion." Renata sips her coffee. "It just looks like it's moving backwards."

"But I feel it," Leigha says. "The vibes around here are just—"

"I'm sure you do," says Renata. In walks Micah, carrying a canvas tote bag containing the burgers.

Leigha says, "I wonder if this is what it feels like if your blood started moving in the other direction."

"Feel what?" He says.

"Off," says Leigha. "And Ren isn't sleeping."

"Oh," Micah says, raising his caterpillar eyebrows. "The boyfriend?"

"Is he moving in?" Leigha asks.

"I would say he's encroaching," says Renata.

"You're not smiling about this."

"I think the Mercury cream is burning my face."

#

After work, Renata is sitting on the rooftop of her apartment building, hanging onto what's left of the daylight by closing one eye at a time, shifting the center point of the clear sky right, then left, right then left. She thinks about what Leigha said earlier about optical illusions being oxymorons, and what she could have meant by that. That perception was an illusion? But obviously. She shifts the sky right, then left, right then left. When she tries to steady both her eyes open, it gives her a shaky feeling. Then, a mass of shadow passes over her. It's Lyle, shading his eyes, messenger bag strap across his chest, holding two to-go cups filled with glowing pinkness.

"Margarita?" he says. "Buy-one-get-one at LoLo's. They even salted the inner rim. With these little sticks."

She sits up and accepts the cup from him, opens its lid, and takes a sip. The tequila pooled on top of the mound of ice nips her tongue.

"God, LoLo's has terrible drinks," she says. "They really just pour shots on flavorless colored ice."

"Does its job," he says, swirling his cup, drinking it back. "Rough day?"

Lyle is an intern at the hospital, in the Developmentally Differently Abled and Resource Challenged wing, formerly known as the Psych Ward. He's an Aphoristic Translator, which means his job is to provide therapists with a proper, concise formulation of truth given the patient's condition that would entail some insight or revelation, leading to their recovery. He more so just sits in an office reading books all day, waiting to be called in, which, he admits, isn't very often. "Medications work better than words," he once said. He's been so stressed lately; he's been talking a lot in his sleep. It's like all the forced thought behind his work throughout his day comes spooling out of him in his sleep. Short, nonsensical phrases, yearning toward something deeper.

Some of her favorites:

"Where we can find a society, there we find lemons also."

"A little obsession is an absolute tango, a great deal of it is to drown."

"Religion is the comedy of pets."

Lately, given her inability to sleep without having the same dream shake her awake, she's been asking him questions. Their silliness soothes her, gets her mind off the track it was going, down some dark tunnel of memory, but sometimes their profundity puts her at ease, like when he said, "Fear is the shadow of hope."

"We had an intense patient today," he says, shaking the ice left in the cup. "Homeless guy. I've seen him around before. Usually just comes in for a bed for the night and the hospital's fruit cups. He's nice. He was telling stories about how he used to deal to Miles Davis."

"Really?"

"Yeah, supposedly he could play, too. Sax, better than Coltrane, he claims. And he would get Miles dope and always try to get into the sessions, like wanting a try-out or something. He never even met him, he says. Miles' guard would just grab a baggie and give him money, and he would stand there sax in hand and say, 'Can I see Miles today?' and the guard would say he's working or something, until one day he had enough and pushed his way through the studio door and confronted Miles and Miles said something to him, something like 'Just because you play, doesn't mean you can blow. You play music, I am music.'"

"Ha, ha. What a loser," she says. "Who says that?"

"Miles Davis."

"So, what?"

"So, nothing. He walked out of the studio, pretty sure he left his saxophone there and never played again. He said he realized the difference between trying to be something and being something, and who he was being, was a dope fiend thinking he could play."

"But wasn't Miles Davis an addict, too?"

"No. He was music."

"So dumb."

"There's a difference."

"Meh."

"Rory later told me the guy was probably lying, anyway."

"So, what else happened? Why intense?"

"Oh, he came in today with a screwdriver in his arm."

#

In the kitchen, Lyle says, "Alexa, play Miles Davis," and bends over the stove, preparing to flip a quesadilla. He's making his famous "fridge-a-dillas" where he chops basically anything he can scrounge up from her fridge and puts it in between two tortillas with cheese. Tonight, it's asparagus, mushroom, kale, sweet corn, and deli-sliced turkey with sharp cheddar. Renata pours some white wine into the remaining pink slush of her margarita cup, tapping her foot on the side of her chair to the music, imagining some guy with a screwdriver in his arm playing alongside the chaotic melody. She enjoys getting lost in these tiny moments of domestication with Lyle; it's them at their best. Him, feigning coolness, twisting and jiving around, dish towel over the shoulder, trying too hard to be slick around the kitchen like some city chef, but is instead goofy and charming, usually forgetting and burning something. Her, pushing down the constant gnawing of the day, having her one daily cigarette near the window, taking in the golden hour of light, admiring Lyle. In these moments, she is no longer herself, not someone who works a job or can't sleep, has nagging back pain; she's not someone with a past or a future, obligated to do or be anything, and the feeling of being a self can dissipate into their shared experience. Isn't this the point of love, to completely dissolve oneself into a union, a single connection? To obliterate the ego, smash the pieces of each other's individuality and mix them all up? There's an entire lifetime in these moments; her and Lyle, forever, nothing existing outside it. These times, however, fade. And quickly. As fast as they came. Usually when Lyle does something she finds completely moronic, like dripping grease from the pan all over the floor, the floor he walks on with his bare feet, then gets into her bed without showering. It's when she's confronted with the image of who he really is that any visions of codependency shatter; capturing the beautiful thing is what gave her scars. And then she's right back to being a self, singular, trapped in her head, hating how loud the music is. Maybe that's what people mean when they talk about relationships being work; it's not with the other person, but in balancing the tug and pull between your own solipsism and selflessness.

\#

They're on the couch, buzzing from the wine, bloated from dinner. They're both on their phones, not talking, and the TV is on, playing a cooking show in the background, flickering against the wall like some art installation. Title: *Modern couple unwinding*. This is the hour they tunnel so far into media all sense of the physical world is lost. The unbearableness of the present. Push it away with memes and videos, news stories and games, the curated glamour of other people's lives. This is what it takes to come back to each other. Only when they are glassy-eyed and dull can they remember what's special between them. What is real. And this isn't anything new. They've talked about it, personal space, awkward silences, when the "honeymoon phase" of their relationship started to fade and they found they were scolding each other for being on their phones more. "A healthy dose of escapism," Lyle said. "People think it's technology-related, that it's just because of our phones. But humans have always done it. It's human nature."

"I'm picturing married couples in the 1600s, sitting next to each other in silence, reading books," she said. "Cave people on opposite sides of their caves, drawing up worlds with their shit, out grazing the land, making shapes out of stars."

"Nature's way of preservation: ignore your spouse to remain in love."

\#

In bed, Lyle is running his fingers over her stomach scars, saying how they feel like worms. Rain is ticking on the fire escape. Renata is getting the feeling of sinking into herself, the one that comes in the early of hours of night. While most people are pulled into sleep, she is pushed out, held up by something. Held up and spun slow-ly by something internal. Her body becomes something else—stiff, clammy, the pores of her skin millions of eyes, blinking, on alert.

"How's High Spiritual these days?" He asks. "You haven't talked about it, no good floaters?"

"Mercury appears to be spinning the other way."

"That's what the nurses say. Going to be crazy tonight, retrograde. I don't get it. Every night in a psych ward is crazy."

"Do you have allergies?" She asks. "Like seasonal."

"Oh yeah. Death by pollen."

"So maybe it's like that. Some people are allergic to planetary phenomena, sensitive to celestial inklings."

"And all I get is a sneeze."

"Must be your first lifetime," she says, rolling on top of him. "That's cute."

Later, Lyle is snoring on his back, and the swelling of her heartbeat is keeping her awake. It fills her ears, has its hands around her neck, her arms. She turns over, leans her nose into his shoulder, and asks him, "What's wrong with me?"

"Autonomy of the body depends on its heteronomy," he says, asleep. "Eat cheese."

#

The next day at work, Leigha is sitting behind the desk massaging the mercury cream into her cheeks, while Micah is cross-legged in his office, opening his fifth chakra. The hum of his throat fills the waiting room of High Spiritual. Renata is next to Leigha, staring straight ahead at the morning fog hovering in the parking lot; she got maybe an hour of sleep last night. She is remembering that in her sleepless daze, lying there, staring at the ceiling, something Lyle said about High Spiritual came to mind. "Talk about escaping reality," he said. "We just now have sexy, more sophisticated ways."

"The indigenous had drugs," she said. "We have float tanks."

"And also drugs," Lyle said.

She got out of bed, and went into the shower; this was about 3 a.m. She turned over the nozzle to the hottest her skin could bare, to melt away the clamminess, and focused the hard stream directly on what Micah would unironically call her "third eye." These middle-of-the-night showers were an insomniac's retreat, where time wasn't made up of seconds but one continuous stream on which her mind could float. Her mind seemed always to be pulling her away, carrying her off. When she considered escapism, she didn't see it as some withdrawal from the world, but rather a thrust into it, like pushing one's own head through a plastic bag, hoping you break through to some other side before suffocating.

"So, I'm not really sure he even likes me like that," says Leigha, snapping Renata's attention back to the moment.

"Hole guy?"

"Yes, well he doesn't live in the hole. It's his parents. They're burrow people."

"Oh yeah, they retired to one. Out in Montana."

"They surface sometimes. To like play golf or whatever," she says. "There's like a whole community of them now."

"Sounds enticing," Renata says. "Like a good fallback plan."

"Here comes your nine o'clock."

#

"You are balled safely in a rain drop. Born of a cloud, a lofty mother, swelling. A ray of sun, a simple push, and your life journey begins now. You and thousands of your brothers and sisters released into the sky, not falling, but bursting toward Earth, a new home. You are free. In this raindrop, you float, hovering, spinning, toward your new bed. There it is, bright green and sheening. Lay back, let the leaf accept you. Roll by, let go, let go, let go. Slide."

#

On her break, Renata is sitting in the grass near the road, looking up at the pylon sign of the shopping mall across the highway. The top sign is for a Target, a few below it are for a burger place, a pizza place, and a hair salon. It's the one beneath those that has her attention, of a Beer & Wine Drive Thru in red neon lettering, but a few of the letters are blacked out, so it reads DIE THRU. She pulls out her phone, snaps a pic, and sends it to Lyle, who responds, "the only way thru is thru."

In the blinding sun, she thinks about Leigha's boyfriend's parents and how nice it must be to live in a hole, to retreat into the ground and slowly give back nutrients, all while being kept alive by various pill shapes and a sack of oxygen set above ground. Maybe this is the only true climate-change prevention. To give up the land, to hide in shame, to allow the Earth to slowly take your body, the way it does trees. Maybe she could start here, roadside, in a pitch of grass. Just lie back and let the ground take her. It could be her first noble act.

"Hey!" She awakes to Leigha calling out, somewhere behind her. "What are you laying near the road for?"

"I'm exhausted," she says.

"That's gross. Come in. Micah is looking for you."

#

If you meet Buddha on the road, kill him, she once read.

The idea had perplexed her. How one needed to kill our own conceptualizations, killing the belief that we understand anything at all. Rid ourselves of idols. If monks sought out to kill the Buddha, then here, in Micah's small, closet office, is a haven for him. Hundreds of them in various shapes and sizes, colors, facial expressions on every shelf, the filing cabinet, his desk; pictures of him on the wall, small statues on the ground. Renata is sitting across from him. Micah makes a bridge with is hands.

"So, little tiff. But before that. Ren, how are you? Inside. Feeling okay?"

"I'm golden," she says.

"Still not sleeping?"

"Well, not really, but it's fine. It happens. I sometimes go through these bouts of insomnia, a few weeks a year. They pass."

Micah's bridge of hands recedes to his pot belly, as he leans back in his chair.

"Well, then. We all have our bouts. So, yeah, the reason I wanted to chat. I'm a little concerned. Your performance around here has been, well, less than High Spiritual. You know, I just got off the phone with Josie Martin, your nine o'clock, and she said it was the worst float experience she's had. That she was expecting utero and you gave her the raindrop experience. And not even a convincing one at that. Your narratives are at a monthly low, tracking 2.3 stars. And Leigha reports a cloud."

"A cloud?"

"Dark energy. You're carrying it around. I can feel it where we sit."

"Okay," she says. "So, what, am I fired?"

"Oh no. No. Absolutely not. I don't believe in firing. I believe in healing. I want to help you. I say we get you in a tank."

#

149

She's never actually been in one of these before. Aside from changing the light filters and setting the temperature gages. But then there's no water in them. She's never laid down in one, with the Pod-mosphere engaged. It's not as dark as she imagined. The water feels dense, like it is holding her up. Her eyes adjust, she can see the texture of the top shell of the tank, hung above her like the night sky, dust star spotted. She thinks of Lyle, looks forward to telling him about this later, how she will probably start to look for other work. When your boss puts you in a sensory deprivation tank to "heal" you, that might be a good indicator to work somewhere else. Maybe unionize, gather Leigha and overtake Lyle. But her floral headband is permanent, with her planetary ointments and vibe-feeling. She is music. Renata would only have to save herself. She can't even remember why she started working here, like it happened to someone else. Someone more naive, a fool, really. Someone broken and looking for something to cling onto, to save herself from drowning in what? Grief? Aimlessness? She remembers being a person who wanted things. Who looked at things like spirituality and wanted something from it. But that was long ago. Now she is a person who just wants some stillness. To lie back, to float, and let the way of things take her wherever they may. Micah's voice comes over the speaker. The water warms, and gently swirls beneath her. A blue hue above.

"You are the ocean," he says. "You are full, vast, deep. You contain all. You are your own ecosystem, sustaining yourself. Chaotic and tranquil, waxing, waning."

She closes her eyes and feels the barrier between her body and the water break down. The muffled exhale of her breath crashes like waves on the shore of her ears. And soon, the Jamaican sky. Preening turquoise. Blinding sun. Her love returns. She remains still.

The Only Thing
Suspicious is You

He is tired of the commute, exhausted by the asphalt smells and diesel fumes wafting into the car, whether through a cracked window or the open-air vent in the engine behind an idling dump truck; the constant stop and go, stop and go, thunking over the massive cracks and deep gorges of unfilled potholes, and worst of it all, the sunken eyes of fellow commuters as they crane their necks, quietly judging. It gets hard seeing the same roadside patches of over-grown crabgrass bending with the wind of traffic, the shores of soot, dirt, and grease that clump up against the concrete median in tidepools of liquid that on some days seem to reflect the sky with the clarity of a great lake and on others spiral in swaths of black tar clouds. The banausic life of the American commuter. Willard Elky, a quiet lonesome resident of the small New Jersey town of Middlesex, is sick of it all, the commuting, yet so detached that, even now on the road, the sunglass-wearing suit in the BMW weaving across three lanes like some sort of stunt driver no longer gives him the slightest bit of a rise, only a wince of disdain for the fact that the prick thinks he is better than everyone else on the road. Maybe he is. Who cares? How mundane it all feels, when even hatred fades into indifference.

In his nine years spent on the road, Willard has learned a few things: that no one gives a shit about you, your car, your lane, your space—that you are not a person in a vehicle but the embodiment of an inconvenience, incapable of assessing the right speeds and rates of acceleration to properly contribute to the flow of traffic. So please do yourself a favor and gravitate towards the shoulder like a tin can kicked to the gutter.

Today, a cloudy spring morning, his Corolla slows to a pocket of traffic near the New Jersey Highway I-78 off-ramp towards N.J. Route 24 and when he comes to a complete stop, Willard's eyes roll away from the windshield out to the barren landscape skirting the soot polluted highway. In the distance, along a row of worn-down factories is a large LED billboard. On it, an advertisement flashes for a new remake of a Broadway musical—*Rent on Ice*. The second ad that flashes is an extradition notice that says "WANTED" in huge red block lettering; beneath that it says, "For Murder" and beside that is a large headshot of the suspect. Willard, gawking over the billboard for too long, almost rear-ends a Subaru. Slamming on his brakes, he takes a breath, then jolts his eyes back to the billboard, thinking the desolate-eyed, low-shaven haired man in picture is him. He wipes his eyes, thinking it can't be and checks back. But when he does, the billboard has flashed onto another advertisement, this one from a Christian media conglomerate asking, "Have you streamed Jesus into your heart yet?"

In the performance of stop and go, stop and go, now

153

just one long stop due to heavy merges on both sides, Willard sketches on the wall of his thoughts his image up on the billboard to consider its plausibility and authenticity, whether or not it could be him; sees his rounded, pudgy face, deep crow's feet at thirty-two, hint of stubble around the silhouette of a smirk that says: I'm a loser with no ambitions and no thoughts or plans—exactly the face he is making on his laminated work I.D. badge. Now that the image has settled, the words Wanted and Murder next to what he believes was his name on a billboard above N.J. I-78, which is the third most populated highway in the state behind the N.J. Turnpike I-95 and N.J. I-80, the early onset symptoms of panic arise in his body—fast heartbeat thumping in his ears, sweaty palms, dry mouth. His thoughts mimic the cartoonish on-screen flashes of the old Batman television series, *Bam!* and *Pow!* being replaced by *What the Fuck!* and *Why!*

Willard's eyes dart back and forth from side mirror to side mirror, and out across the traffic-ridden interstate, then above to the cloudless oceanic sky, looking for police helicopters, private investigators in trench coats, or some pedestrian vigilante nearby who had just saw the same billboard he did and recognized him as the suspect. At this moment of shifty paranoia, a man with a ripped black T-shirt with tan and white spots all over it crosses in front of his Corolla's front bumper carrying a large tin coffee can and a saxophone slung over his back. He's wearing crusty stiff black denim shorts that he could tell were once pants now cut at mid-thigh revealing a tattoo that due to the skin pigmentation of the man's leg is hard to make out, but Willard thinks looks like a lion's head. Willard watches with a clarity that only heightened awareness from intense anxiety and paranoia brings; it's almost as if he could feel the man breathing or hear the man's thoughts as he sets up a makeshift seat using cardboard that was already there in the median of I-78's offramp onto Rt.-24. Willard suspects this man to be a plant, some federal agent who will get the go-ahead to take Willard out at any second, but for now sits coolly on the cardboard seat leaning against the aluminum column of the exit sign with black Ray-Ban sunglasses, saxophone in hand, playing the intro notes to what Willard recognizes as George Michael's "Careless Whisper," the clichéd go-to for street saxophonists.

Beautiful music aside, Willard is stuck in the middle lane between the two merging lanes in a gridlock. There's no escape. A car over, a woman in a Tesla removes a portable make-up bag from her glove box and begins to bat at her eye lashes with mascara. In front of her, a man in an Acura sedan closes his eyes in a non-forceful or clasped way, just allowing them to lightly cover the convexes of his eyes—they even flutter a little bit as he takes deep, exaggerated breaths, looking like he is leading a class on meditation; he, Willard thinks, seems to also have a lot going on. The guy in the Subaru in front of Willard pouts and angles his maw in the rearview mirror as he makes circular passes over and under his chin with an electric razor. Someone in a bright orange compact Jeep Wrangler edges in front of Willard, thinking it seems, that somehow his car will fit in the ~8inches between Willard's bumper and the Subaru's back bumper and that this lane magically is moving faster than the others or going anywhere at all; the Jeep also has a high mount snorkel extension at the front and what looks to be a kayak paddle strung up on three hooks at the top of the back window of its vinyl coated soft top, which Willard can't help but smirk at thinking of the guy driving directly into a lake. All these people, especially the woman in the Volkswagen Jetta to his left who seems to be harmonizing with a song over the radio in an overly dramatic, drunk-karaoke-ish way, Willard thinks, or rather assumes, are federal agents moving in on him; why else would they all be actively avoiding making eye contact with him? It's this line of thinking that makes him mute his stereo, grip the steering wheel tight, and cautiously observe everyone around him, hoping that he can just make it to work.

Willard works as an eCommerce coordinator for a fortune 500 company and has been thinking for a while now that it is killing him. "The air," he says, to no one. "I'm allergic to the air in this place." He's been in the same low-level position for nine years and he spends every day doing the same thing over and over again: sneezing and scratching his eyes, and sneezing, onboarding more products, and sneezing, and dying, and dying, and dying. He is reminded of this long torturous corporate march to death every time he parks his car in the same spot he does every day—the one near the large hole in the wooden fence along the woods at the back of the lot, where just enough wilderness creeps through to remind him that not all of the world has been paved over or littered in advertisements or built up into shiny steel office buildings where everything inside is made of plastic and laminated MDF. His issues with Capitalism now feel fully realized, as if it was some genetic implantation that took some time to develop; where he once was able to forego its cost to his human spirit—the spending, the wasting, the spending, the wasting—for hope at some distant comfortable future, like his parents', he now feels lied to, taken advantage of, which is why every morning he stands in front of that hole in the fence, a portal to rustling thicket covered in a blaze of browning leaves and century old trees whispering secrets to each other through the mycelia underfoot; he imagines true freedom as when you can no longer be advertised to, not even by your own thoughts.

Isn't it strange, among the array of car horns varying in

pitch mixing intermittently with the saxophonist who seems to know only the main riff of "Careless Whisper," traffic at a standstill, the sky resembling the soft hue of a blue jay's back, Willard would find himself on a wanted sign? For murder of all things? Of all days, such a sunny beautiful blank sheet of a day to be wanted for murder, one where Willard would usually drive straight to work nodding and talking back to Big Bob Odendotter, host of The Morning Pitch, Central Jersey's premiere baseball podcast, nodding and laughing and arguing with the voice coming through the stereo, gulping down his twenty-four ounce quadruple shot hazelnut latte with two extra packets of sucralose—that's what it takes to beat the commute at times, to fully disengage from pavement-level reality and not think about the fact that you are literally a cog in a machine, albeit a slow-moving one; it's about the ability to just tune out the idea that you are on your way to a job that you hate—not even hate, really, but spiritually disdain—a job in which you have been willfully employed for ~3,285 days. That's the kicker, what gets Willard hung up and on the verge of a good knee-hug-cradling cry—he is there willfully. It's not masochistic, because in that type of duality, there's at least pleasure in the pain and humiliation. No, this is a deeper, complex fault in the inner system of his brain, or, dare he think it, some generational brainwashing that's been decades in the making to get someone to live a life in which day after day they continue doing what they loath.

After moving into the right lane to edge around the Jeep Submarine, Willard can see the root of all the traffic about the length of ten cars ahead—a construction zone set up on the shoulder with cones and large dump trucks with orange signs posted on their rear cab gates stating: **Caution: Pick Up Crew Ahead**. Along the line of cones are police cars and vans with cages in their windows with their reds and blues flashing on their roofs, not swirling as in the case of being in pursuit, but just flickering on and off as some sort of alert. It's there that Willard sees the line of men in orange jumpsuits with cloth sacks strung over their backs and long wooden sticks with plastic needles on the ends. About twice as many cops per orange jumpsuit watch closely with what appear to be shotguns as the men bend and pluck pieces of trash out from the tangled tall grass of the shoulder. Most of the men are Black, some are Latino, Willard suspects, and his paranoia is diverted for a second to make room for a sadness at the revelation that all the cops with guns are white. But the sadness evaporates as soon as the image of the billboard appears again in Willard's mind and he sees himself in one of the inmates on the side of the road, imagines what it could feel like being chained at the ankles, sweat pooling on the back of his sun-drenched neck, being surveilled by guards with deeply wounded egos living out some enforcer fantasy ready at the helm to react at any excuse you give them to fill your chest with bullets to prove once and for all that they are above you. Willard's breath now feels as if it were escaping him, that he was only exhaling and unable to inhale anything at all except the real fear that he is being tracked and monitored right now by law enforcement. He didn't kill anyone, he knows this, but due to the ongoing stories he hears of Black men still being wrongfully convicted of crimes they didn't commit, he knows that the accusation itself makes his innocence nearly irrelevant.

To cope with this potentiality, Willard's mind dives into it. He starts playing a reel of scenarios in which being arrested and convicted for murder would be totally manageable if taken one thing at a time, the way one is nervous before starting a new job, but once there and in the day-to-day of it and after a short adjustment period, one looks back and wonders why they were even nervous in the first place. He sees himself going through all the processes, the physical exam, having to strip down naked and spread his butt cheeks for the guard whose lips are permanently flattened in a smug grin; the psych evaluation, with questions designed to confuse him and shape his mind as a type of map for crime being all but guaranteed to have happened—Oh, we see you excelled at the extremely violent sport of football as a youth, and so on. The satisfying confirmation of his place in this world. Then the day-to-day, the solitude, the time and space to read and think, and exercise—Willard, with mild body dysmorphia since a teen, likes the idea of having nothing to do but work out, and even indulges in the image of him yoked to the nines, walking the cellblocks in the same way he once walked the halls at Concordia High School. Of course, there would be prison yard social games (probably not too much different than the ones he experiences at the office with male colleagues but with the masculine ego ramped up to the max) but Willard would smile through it all from a dissociative place knowing in his heart's truth of his innocence; in fact, maybe it would be possible if some grace were to be found within himself by sitting in a eight foot by eight foot cell knowing that it was not he who acted in evil, but a corrupt system; that he was like the deer of truth in a forest of lies. Plus, three square meals a day and a bed to sleep in.

It's in this reverie where Willard latches onto some sort of peace, and feels his body start to relax in the great crawling traffic on I-78. He even slightly revels in this fantasy of being locked up and not having to ever go back to his corporate job and never having to deal with the morning routine race to find the perfect spot in the football field shaped parking lot, usually being cut off by luxury cars with ironic license plate tags, to settle for his faraway spot near the hole in the fence; the nodding and tonally flat non-warm greeting from Giles, the front desk security guard who checks every person's I.D. badge as they enter the office; the walks, past rows of desolate cubicles, to achieve his 5,000-step daily goal, on which lately, while walking Willard has noticed the cubes have remained empty, meaning that maybe The Company is under some clearing house initiative to remove staff or maybe the department was moved to another floor; the occurrences of small talk happening at intersections of cubicles, especially on Mondays ("How was your weekend?") and Fridays ("Thank God It's Friday") or after big sporting events ("Did you see the game?") that Willard, even though he sees this as the only extension of humanity, often tries to avoid by appearing he is in a rush to his desk, which he usually is due to the twenty-four-ounce quadruple shot hazelnut latte with two extra packets of sucralose on his drive in that has now hardened and sunk into his stomach, ready to be defecated at any second; the morning anxiety of removing his witch-hazel soaked hemorrhoidal care wipes from his messenger bag at his desk with no one hearing, smelling, or seeing him as he bundles it up into his fist and walks down to the smaller bathroom in his wing, taking a chance at one of the two stalls rather than walking further to the main bathroom on his floor with twelve stalls, which he would easily find an open stall but comes with a higher chance of seeing a colleague who puts out their hand for a shake or, worse, asks, "Will, what's that bundled up in your hand?" He certainly will not miss the thin sheet of waxy film shaped like a toilet seat that once Willard properly rips and applies with gentle caution to the top of the toilet seat with unidentifiable liquid or little curly hairs on it gets sucked down into the flushing toilet as he set off

the motion sensor flushing mechanism by turning to un-
buckle his belt and lowering his pants too quickly, having
to do this half-naked dance with the sensor, which leads
to a minimum of two thin sheets of waxy film daily and
telling himself that tomorrow he will remember to remove
his pants first before applying the seat cover to the seat;
onboarding products Willard thinks are ruining society,
by making people lazier, more reliant on the convenience
of machines like the little clicker he recently added, the
"OptoFridge," a remote that opens the door to your refrigerator and controls the inner lights to your preference and
can highlight the different food groups according to the
color code of your choice—for instance the veggie drawer
can light up green and the meat shelf can light up red, or
you can black out certain parts of the fridge you don't want
others, i.e. your kids or silly husband, to see, such as the
sweets or the fresh cake or pie you baked but is being saved
for a special occasion. He's not going to miss eating lunch
in his car to avoid social interaction with his colleagues
who seem to be completely blind to this cynical underbelly
of corporate life, who in fact, seem to indulge in it with
their wireless charging pads for their gadgets, coffee heat-
ing pads, small fans, and bright desk lamps that help cure
their seasonal affective disorder, resulting in a constant
dreadful hum that masks the whooshing exhaust of the
dirty air vents overhead, which Willard has to tune out
with wireless noise-cancelling headphones; won't miss the
meetings in the conference rooms which some call "fish
bowls" that have recessed LED lighting in the ceiling that
are way softer on the eyes than the usual track fluores-
cent lighting you'll find over the standard blocks of cubicles which some speculate cause chronic migraines and
a sore, vague heat felt only in the eyes, but when lit, the
conference room LEDs, often in midafternoon give off

the feeling of the early morning compared to the brighter and warmer sunlight outside, which gives you a cognitive scramble and resonates as a sudden sleepiness in addition to the three o'clock slump, which is why it is recommended to schedule meetings in the morning, or at least provide some sort of nutritional snack to your team if holding a meeting in the afternoon.

Maybe jail will be better, he thinks, while noticing the traffic ahead starting to break up, which means soon he will be on his way. The billboard is still clear in his mind, but now it seems like some sort of outlet from this mundane life that he's found himself in; a life in which a company offers access to an on-campus gym and meditation/prayer room, but also condemns the use of such utilities during work hours, but rather, instead, encourages you to remain on campus for at least twelve to fourteen hours a day to include these extracurricular activities into your daily routine and participate in peer bonding within the walls of the corporate headquarters rather than say, at a bar, where the likelihood of misconduct is far greater; a life in which sitting at a desk for eight hours a day, ~40 hours a week, results in rolled shoulders, a stiff slouched neck which some people call "tech neck," lower back issues, and other long-term health complications medical professionals have begun to equate with a lifelong habit of smoking; a life in which you must keep the real you, and any inkling of who might really be, like deep down, hidden from those around you, those who in return you need to see the slightest inkling of that depth from, but can't, it's like ships with their signals off, drifting further and further apart.

Outside the car, heat settles over the blacktop, which Willard feels gently rising up against his forearm dangling out the window. The sun casts an erratic spritz of light that when he squints one eye at, takes the shape of the spiny brown gumballs that lay at the bed of some of the trees around the man-made foam walking path at the office. A flock of crows are lined up on a thick telephone wire, loom-

ing over the carcass of a deer smashed into the concrete median, all but just twenty yards from the saxophonist, who
happens to be now on a smoke break. Willard looks back
to the median, studies it, sees how rigid its concrete form
is, yet, there are parts of it that have broken away, leaving
cliffs of chalky rock and sponge-like pours and twisted
rebar piercing the surface; Willard always forgets the im-
permanence of infrastructure, that eventually roots rise
and crack through pavement, that nature retreats and
takes back. Shifting his eyes toward the shoulder, Willard catches a glimpse of a smile on one of the inmate's
faces who, as he bent to pick up what looked to be the
bottom half of a stroller, one that Willard undoubtedly
has onboarded to the site before, a squirrel had fallen
onto its back from a high branch, thudding on the grass,
and scurrying away as if in embarrassment. Willard feels
to be totally removed from the anxiety as he considers
the possibility of being convicted for a crime he didn't
commit being equivalent to a life spent in a corporate
office; here he notices that the image of the billboard in
his mind is less vivid, which completely evaporates when
looking back up at the actual billboard to see someone
named William Ellers wanted for murder. Willard sur-
prises himself how—and most people would not buy this
at all––how maybe all it takes is a shift in perspective
to make a cubicle feel like a cell and a corporate office
feel like a prison and vice versa; try telling one of the
guys picking up trash in the shoulder right now, Willard thinks, and see how many bruises and broken bones
you get. But still, one should try. One should maybe try
to keep such a perspective, that within us all lies some
deep untouched place in which you could occupy and not
let society get its gross systemic hands on; it could be a
place that is beyond time and space, hidden from reckless

guys in BMWs or Submarine Jeeps, hidden from people like Martha Tate, the director of eCommerce, Willard's boss, who has rotten gray teeth and coughs out passive aggressive orders to Willard through his team lead Tiana, like how he shouldn't be seen reading in the cafeteria, regardless if it was his state mandated fifteen minute break or not, reading with your ankle resting on your other knee just plain looks bad, (Willard notes how many people spend way more than fifteen minutes in the cafeteria staring at their phones or on walks around the track, but don't get him started on that either); who knows, maybe that tiny space within oneself could be accessed, where every negative occurrence is a lesson and every positive is a reaffirmation of that inner peace, Willard hopes, noting the needle finally inching past 10 m.p.h. on his speedometer's LED screen, the sun cracking like yolk through dense gray clouds.

Cracked

Someone who was once famous, but not so much anymore, said, "Every whole person has ambitions, initiatives, goals," about a boy who was very particular and wanted to press his lips to every square inch of his own body. This is not about said boy, but a different boy, a peculiar boy who had never read that story and whose goal was to crack every joint, every ligament, every air pocket and poppable piece of cartilage in his body. The boy was seven.

The origins of this habit, which he simply called "cracking" were unknown to him, but if given some thought he might be able to discern two instances in his young life that would have acted as trigger events—as in unrelated, seemingly random phenomenon that took place in distinct separate moments of time, the way a few talks behind closed doors in one nation and one act of violence in another coordinate with bubbling protests in a third-world country, inevitably leading to a world war. That's what this was for the boy, a war with his body, a war with tightness and pressure. The two random and insignificant events that led to this obsession, if brought to the front of his memory and studied, would be as such:

1. Driving on I-80 heading south in his mother's mini-van, probably somewhere in Virginia—the strip of VA that feels endless—looking out at the passing nothingness and earnest poppy billboards of advertisements, remnant of the '70s, from the back seat, the then-three or -four-year-old boy had an urge (probably subconscious, probably out of boredom) to squeeze his index finger down into his palm until the metacarpophalangeal joint, commonly known as the base knuckle, suddenly popped.

2. Since the knuckle popping car incident, the boy began bending, squeezing, twisting, clenching, extending, contorting and pretzel-ing each of his fingers until he achieved loud pops and high cracks along each of his metacarpophalangeal, proximal interphalangeal, and distal interphalangeal joints, which led to frustration, swollen fingers, and—inevitably—boredom. That was until almost a year later when the boy was four or five and had started playing recreational tee-ball down at Dawson Park every Tuesday and Thursday. At his first practice on an especially wet April evening, he joined the team of boys and girls for stretches. The first of which was a Lumbar Rotation Stretch—lying supine, arms spread, right leg over the left making the shape of a capital P. At first, he felt stupid being crossed and soaked on the grass of the outfield, but after a gentle (probably subconscious) lean into the pose, his spine rattled like a string of firecrackers, consequentially blowing his young mind. Later, he would do research on the Internet to discover he had cracked from the L3 or L2 vertebrae of his lumbar spine (lower) all the way up to the T6 or T5 vertebrae range of his thoracic spine (middle), becoming obsessed with the idea that each of his vertebrae were labeled with numbers and letters, wondering if the rest of his joints were labeled, because if so, he could treat his body like a game of Connect-the-Dots, just with cracks instead of ink.

By the age of seven, the boy was cracking pretty much all day aside from periods of non-cracking to let his joints fill with air, which he liked to imagine as bubbles filling each crevice of bone and tissue. From the time he woke up, he had a routine of cracking that he would cycle through. First, he started with the back. Supine, he would lift one leg over the other with his arms out and jerk back, twisting upward; this would cause a cracking sensation similar to the baseball stretching incident, a lineage of cracks, but sometimes only a deep thud or worse, no cracks, would come and he would feel a sense of tightness swelling in his back, which would mean that was a bad day. Next came each finger in six different ways, followed by each toe in three different ways; he found that his toes were harder to crack, because instead of having three joints like the fingers, the toes only had one, the interphalangeal joint.

Lastly came the neck. Sitting up in bed, he didn't crane his neck slowly, as some videos on YouTube had suggested. Instead, he whipped his ear towards his shoulder, getting a consistent slash of cracks on each side. When once witnessed by his mother at breakfast, she had said, "That looks like you're going to snap your own damn neck."

Which he did by the winter of that year.

The boy was now ten and after three crack-less years due to snapping his C2, C3, and C4 cervical vertebrae in his neck, he felt tight like all hell and ready and motivated to release every sac and joint that had filled with air and fluid since his accidental injury. He began watching more YouTube videos titled, "Epic Cracks" for inspiration and within three months of having his neck cast off, he was back to cracking every vertebra and joint in his back, neck, fingers, and toes.

His mother, bless her big southern heart, started to get

167

worried about the boy again when he would grow agitated at not being able to crack certain parts of himself. He would tantrum—crying, swinging fists, throwing his clothes off at a jammed knuckle that wouldn't budge. She considered taking to him to see the town therapist to have her run some tests, as she saw all this cracking as a possible manifestation of some internal strife; what her mother, the boy's grandmother, would call, "The Devil's Innards." But she was not her mother; like her father, she didn't believe in the devil or the psychiatric arts. So, she let the boy fuss and pop and crack, figuring it was just a phase.

The cracking seemed to mean more to the boy than just a routine or phase because by the time he was twelve he had learned how to contort himself in all strange ways to crack more and more advanced spots in his frail, thin body. He would snap his wrists back like he was revving a motorcycle for a good crack; twist his arms to crack his elbow and shoulder joints; spread his legs out in a horse stance and thrust his hip to each side until both flexors popped; spin his ankles like pinwheels; press his hands along his shins, forearms, ribcage, collar bones, and femurs looking for cracks; collapse his knees, tucking both legs underneath him, bounce until each gave the sound of victory. Craaaaaack.

One night, after the boy had used his desk chair to dig into his lumbar spine for a few good cracks, the boy felt a strange new pressure in the center of his chest. It had felt like gas had seeped in and was causing him to feel bloated and tight. He felt that he needed to crack there. Unsure of how he could get it done, he first pressed his chest up against the side of his bed frame. Instead of a crack, the wooden post just dug into his sternum and made the pain worse. He then went over to his medicine ball, purchased from Amazon, and laid on his back and stretched while gently rolling back and forth, but the pressure just would not budge. Next, he thought he could press down each vertebra in his sternum using his thumb, the way he had discovered places to crack on the top of his foot. But, with each press, he felt more and more pain, until finally, in agitated surrender, the boy stretched his arms far-out and reached each behind his back with a jolt, until the tips of his fingers nearly touched in a Sistine-like way. Alas, a massive crack shuddered through his chest and released a wave of tingles through his ribs, up across his shoulder blades, and down his arms to his fingertips. He fell back onto the floor, frozen like a mannequin that had been pushed over. A wave of cold sensitivity rushed through him and soon he felt nothing, just stillness, free of pressure and tightness. He had done it; he had cracked his way into eternal bliss, never having to feel anything ever again.

Thrownness

Local Hero Saves Handicap Neighbor from Burning House; decides to remain nameless.[1]

---

1 Born into this world of terror and flame, of a hot spiritual cleansing—is this not how to start over? Burn away your materials, the objects of meaning tying you down to your past? It is never a choice, is it? For either party involved. He, a man, but maybe in this moment he is everything but a man—no, maybe a spirit, an angel, better yet: he is his mother, saintly, or he is his sister, both of whom have saved, sacrificed, led honest good lives. It's possible he is an animal—a beast of sorts—here, in this house, to hunt. But why here? Oh, prey, yes. Hot food, indeed. Shall he wait? Shall he take a seat, wrap napkin like bib around neck and be served? Such heinous thoughts—now? Of all times, especially? Okay, maybe he is just a man, fine. But he knows nothing of the life he lived before the one he is living now; here, in this inferno. Was he a good man? An iron worker? An oceanographer? Perhaps, simply, a good neighbor? One hopes. Or maybe he was worse: a criminal, a czar, an Adman, God no, a warmonger? Could he justify such past lives? For what is reincarnation but an all-paid vacation to somewhere you have earned? Look around, Bucko. House in flames. Oh, shit. Lord have mercy. What about her? What life did she lead to get here? In wheelchair. Scorched house. Belongings burning. It is her things being ruined after all; he just showed up. Yes, he is the hero; that's all heroes do, they show up. Be present. But maybe he is the villain; it's possible he set the fire. For what? Insurance? Fame? Malevolence? For what is a hero but a villain with better intentions? But her, through smoke and flame and ash and—was that a cat? Is she the victim? Victim to what? Him? Can't be. Why must man swoop in and save? If she, victim, could just see that she could be the hero, too, he would be relieved of such a predicament. Instead of crossing the house and lifting her up like some macho man's man, erupt out into the world, her in arms, to what? Flashing cameras? Applause? Another victory for man. Ego flattered. No, he could be kind, compassionate, allow her to save herself. Don't. Explain. Anything. This is a bad time

170

Rules For Escaping

for moral ethics. Okay, maybe he will just show her how to escape from where he is, across the room. "Roll yourself to me!" He yells—at what?—a wall of fire, through which he can only see the woman practically through a pinhole, panting, poor thing. He thinks, Okay, suck it up dummy, she needs you. How long has he been here thinking? With all this heavy smoke looming, he hopes not long; smoke in lungs and all that. Never smoked a cigarette in his life. Would developing lung cancer from this moment be what the woman on the television calls "Beautiful irony?" Oh, time. Has he wasted it? The woman is still alive, he knows, hopes. Must do something. With a fractional knowledge of all things, especially science or math, ugh, he figured in a moment like this, time would go super speed, Zoomo Kiddo, the way it feels in his memory of the time his father got him that scooter and he and Jimmy, Petey, Frankie, Al, and Bill-Boy blasted down the hill outside of St. Mary's Church. Sacred ground for such speed, in a flash, right into the hands of Jesus. Well, really, Father Pap not Jesus, saying, "Boys, can't you take that horseplay somewhere else?" Happened that fast. Here, now, not so much. Time feels stretched out real thin, so thin that everything is still, even the fire, it is glass. Shall he break through? But on this plane of existence the woman is moving further away, or he away from her. She is shrinking. Where you going, Old May? He wants to say. But can't. Breath is fading. He's in motion towards her; in fact, he is running, flailing—thin, lanky thing—shooting across the living room like light. He's making a scene! Knocking over side tables, dishes, cups, saucers, kitchen table, chairs, all like cardboard cut-outs rising up and orbiting him, dashing for the woman in her chair, the queen upon her thrown. He gets to her. "Your majesty," he says. She smiles. Eyes in shock. What comes after? Same as before, one could say. Nothingness. He'll be thrown into a new life, changed by this one; the lawn will still need to be cut. And for her, if she makes it out alive, she too, changed. By what? Him. And maybe a brief recollection of this chaotic life they lived together will come again in dreams or déjà vu or manifest in a silent understanding between them—a smile and nod will do—if they ever pass each other again, as strangers on the street, as neighbors, as lovers or friends, as two bees in the same colony, two orchids blooming side by side sharing roots, as two neutrons coming together, colliding, swirling in flame, spewing light and heat until total depletion, where they would become forever entwined in darkness, just like the place from which they came.

171

Field Notes from the Mud

They woke me in the night by grinding their teeth next to my ears. Their thin torsos stretched onto the walls and ceiling in black silhouettes as if they were dancing around a flame in a cave. Soon, I was in the kitchen being scolded for failing them as a father.

"You're done," Jaden, my youngest, said, flexing his seven-year-old upper body muscles. He looked like a small chimpanzee with the body hair of an allover dinosaur print footie. My oldest, Laney, stood next to him with her arms crossed, pouting with a sinister fourteen-year-old stare from behind a veil of curly dark bangs, shaking her head as if I were a disappointment. My wife Kora entered as soon as they started banding my wrists behind my back with their iPhone chargers.

"What are his crimes?"

Jaden removed a piece of scrap paper from his T-Rex embroidered chest pocket. I saw it was written in crayon as he passed it to Laney.

"We hereby accuse the defendant of the following fatherly crimes," she said. "Over consumption of the bagels; stinginess of attention; sharp word arrows directed at Mom; smelly feet; uncleanly bathroom habits; moody temper; beastly grunts; psychic abuse; barefoot basement walking; colossal snoring; shower-time rushing; high alcohol intake; judging eyes; despair slouching..."

"Please," I said.

"And first-degree hope slaughter."

"Hope slaughter?" I said.

"Your reign," Jaden said, twirling his little league bat in his hand. "Is over. You will dampen our dreams no more."

"Kora," I said.

"And how do we find him?" She said.

"Guilty!" They shouted, before Jaden clipped my knees and they dragged me into the forest beyond our yard to bury me up to the neck in mud.

This happens from time to time. My family convicts me of my crimes and sentences me to time buried in the ground. They send me here to rediscover listening, they say, that I deserve to be punished whenever I become a fascist of the house, when I ignore them for the dictatorial voice in my head. I get it. I am a human being and sometimes I can get stressed and so caught up in words, I forget I have a body, forget I have an obligation to others through action and speech. There have been many times when I've given up the English language, expressing my thoughts in guttural murmurs, opinionated drivel, and have to leave my home at Kora's request; it's more of a recommendation than an order, as she understands that sometimes second-rate speech is the only way to let the pain out. Now it seems that I have gone too far, yet again. But hope slaughter? Come on.

Being the fourth time that my family has hog-tied me and buried me in the forest, I've started to become aware of certain things. There is a silence that comes from being this low to the ground, from being immersed up to your neck in nature. It's a silence that cloaks you, the way one feels the locked tongue that comes from being non-bilingual in a foreign land. When one reaches this level of silence, observational research is only natural. Here, driven into the mossy bed of the forest like a spike, I am mute; I am a stranger to nature's voice. Trying to listen and decipher is the only way I can shut up internally and remember how I used to be.

I was a person once. Grotesquely male, a scientist with esteem and accolade, a home that kept out the bears and thieves. I once had visions of being great, someone who time would carry along holding up their picture. But all that went away ever since my first time out here in my hole. My crimes that time were as such: shrewdness, impatience, intrusion. Next thing, I was bloodied, bruised—Jaden was more liberal with the bat then—and above both of those things, stubborn as all hell. You can't put me down, I thought. I am your father for fuck's sake. A man of my stature, my acclaim. But you'd be surprised at the will of the disenfranchised; and Jaden has a mean swing for his age. I'm kind of proud.

My first reaction to this process was to say screw Jaden and his court. If they knew any better, they'd hold a trial out here in the law of nature; see how my fatherly crimes measure up to say, the male grizzly bear, who eat their young. I've never done anything that bad, I thought. So, I got loud a few times and bullied him into tight corners of shame, but all fathers do that; and yeah, I blistered his hands from making him grip a bat for long enough to learn how to hit a laced ball, but sorry for trying to implement some skill set into his defective DNA lineage (my side, not Kora's). I remember thinking it's not like I stretched him out on a table and snipped at all of his fearchords with pliers like my father did.

But, on that first night, as I writhed around and tried

to shimmy free of my dirt straitjacket, all I could see were Laney's weepy eyes as she told me that this needed to be done, that they couldn't take me being in the house anymore. I trusted her, my teenage daughter, who always was obsessed with brutal honesty; it's no shocker that she smiles when reading out my list of crimes. I feel that she's the one I've really let down. For no reason other than what is a failure to understand. She is not like Jaden, some beast of my seed that I know inside and out, an animal like me who needs to be tamed. She is much like Kora, an ethereal spirit. Which is why the only way I knew how to love her was to let her be; to not let the microscope of study affect her behavior in any way. She would call me aloof or distant, but I would call it crown shyness, a phenomenon observed in some tree species, in which the crowns of fully stocked trees do not touch each other, forming a canopy with channel-like gaps between them, almost like one tree's branches are haloing the others, showing what love and care can look like with space, to inhibit the spread of one's own disease or leaf-eating insect larvae to the other. I cannot say it any more clearly.

That first time they left me here for two days, and when I returned home, I was changed, broken even. After each time I am buried, it seems that I then do fine in the house for a few weeks at a time, reveling in my own obsessions, not harassing my family by existing, but then I start to unravel and become caught up in the motions of the identity of "fatherhood." I begin to get restless in my body and act out with ridiculous phrases, or sometimes with scolding silence. I bang on doors, slam dishes down into the sink, bark orders. I see my children as my workers, my wife as my subordinate. It's as if I forget what I saw on that first night of burial and relive the man-of-the-house cycles that have been passed down through generations.

For my father and grandfather, it was alcohol that helped them; for my great grandfather, it was work. For me, it's a judicial system, where my kids are the prosecutors, my wife is the judge, and the ground is my prison.

I'm getting thirsty. When my family banishes me to this excavation of mud and sorrow, they do so with no food or water, planting me in the earth with hopes that true nourishment will allow for growth. I can't blame them for wanting a better Dad. I'm actually jealous I hadn't thought of this for my old man, put him on trial. My way of internalizing his behavior and quietly murdering him in my mind had only landed me in years of expensive therapy. Is your child ending up in therapy the marker of failing as a parent? Or is it the marker of succeeding? Raising a person to be self-aware enough to get help and not retreat to vices is no easy task; perhaps, I should call my dad and thank him. So, what does it mean when your kids feel authoritative enough to persecute you?

I am hungry and want to scream out to my wife, but I know successful fasts start with the ceasing of speech, the shutting of the mouth, then what follows is a muting of the mind once you get past desire's antics. All in the name of experiencing clear thought (an oxymoron). Consider what I'm doing to be a plugging into the ground like I'm a Universal Serial Bus downloading what I can store from the network of mycelia all around me. Trying to access an essential file to override the fathervirus that exists within me. This Earth-buried, frostbitten-hair-looking organism is the epitome of cross-platform technology, sharing nutrition, like information, from trees and plants, eradicating pollution from the soil and water. A perfect system. It's what our Internet aspired to, but that is made up of language, therefore impure. With every 1, a 0; with every thought, its adverse, a pollution of thought.

Speaking of, that first night is when I made a discovery. I've found something out here in my forest-cell and every time I come back here, I am forced to relearn it. Call it an order of things. I should say that when I'm here, assuming my rightful position in the ground, scribbling into this thoughtjournal to rediscover my place in existence, that there is a level of danger to my mental-work. It's in the lined blankness of this natural medium where the beast of true language lives; I better tread lightly, as to not waken it. We have not been able to capture and share it without the use and filter of physical tools, like our brain parts and mouths, pens and paper, a process that taints the message before it's even received. If this were to get out as-is, I would be persecuted, perhaps injected with a lethal dosage of media, where my findings would be erased from memory for eternity.

You see, it's to my human perspective (another oxymoron) that everything seems random, uncoordinated, chaotic—this, I suspect, is the ego's doing; shuffling around the pieces just to give me a puzzle to solve, so to speak—but when I look closely around, from where I am buried, I see the way everything works in relation to the other, how each species of plant, animal, and insect depend on communication to coexist, leaving me feeling left out like how I felt at what was once called "home," utterly useless, except for allowing the theft of carbon from my lungs. And now after witnessing the order of nature, life is in disarray and I am no longer able to uphold the illusions of control that is essential of a successful body. So, now I consider myself to be just a perspective. I'm no longer a husband, a father, a man, or even a being—only a skin vessel through which ideas can pass. Kora, my wife, trained astrologist, vegan, yogi tinged slightly with privilege, believes this is just a phase of aging crisis, but I am not as knowing as she; her spirit seems to be born of something I cannot understand. She tells me I am lost in the realm of thoughtspeak and that the breath is a doorway out. "Some say that the breath is the origin of language," I told her, which made me wonder why every time I come to this place to meditate, all I hear are my own cries for help.

How can I learn in the forest when my head is full of fear? All these noises—creaking, breathing, cooing, snapping. When I'm here in my hole, I am reminded of the power of words in a "family." My first word as a newborn was "Shhh," a shushing sound, already craving silence to serve my thoughts in the presence of expecting parental eyes. They stood around my crib, adulating my vulnerable self, unaware of how tainted I've already become from their judgments. It was from then on that I had no hope. Lacey's first words were incriminating vowels. "You," she'd say. I'd ask, What's the matter sweetie? "You. You." Jaden's first words were an erasure, as if I never existed. "Mama. Ma-ma." Is language only our own interpretation of speech? When I listen to the forest speaking to me, all I hear are threats. How moronic of us to assume we were the speaking ones. That somehow the outpouring of petty thought, impulsive motive, lust-driven emission, and delusional hopespeak would pin us atop God's hierarchy; God is silent because she probably knows that we would try to topple her throne if she ever talked back. Meanwhile, as we spray each other with speech and fill each other's minds with the toxic sludge of opinion, there is silent oration going on around us, at all times, in total harmony. So, the question is no longer if plants can talk, but if we are deaf.

"Hello," I say to the Hazel Alder plant beside me.

Like God, it doesn't answer. Does the plant know it's being spoken to? Does it know it's being eaten? Does it even care? When in danger, I yell for help, for God, for my mother. When maize is being attacked by beet armyworms, they release chemical clouds that attract wasps to lay eggs in the caterpillar's bodies; the enemy of your enemy is your friend. A plant responds to touch internally, biochemically analyzing the feeling to shape a future behavior, but when I touch a leaf, I feel nothing and understand even less. Now, who's more efficient? See? I'm doing it again, the sardonic thoughtspeak of a shattered ego.

The void of night has drawn close. It must be around three a.m. of I don't know what day. I'm immersed in the ambient sound of chirps, clicks, and buzzing. What the insects say is I'm unwelcome. That the absence of light will be my downfall. But I don't care. I'm starting to miss my family. Deep in the dirt I feel fibers of hair not of my own tingling up from my shins to my torso. It feels like one creature with thousands of tiny legs having its way with me. It's not as if I don't deserve it, I've done unspeakable things. But who hasn't? Awful is in our genetic make-up. It's how we prospered, how we eventually acquired the moral sense to condemn ourselves. And I certainly do. I just don't know how to explain any of this to Kora, Laney, and Jaden; language fails guilt and shame. But maybe it's not anything I can say but do. Even better, maybe it is something that I can just be. Instead of ruining my chances of being a true-father by speaking to them through words, maybe I can embody compassion and love, something transferable through looks and consented huddling. What if the best kind of Dad you can be is one devoid of conviction?

In the distance, I spot a coyote clearing bark chips, grass, and dirt to burrow for the impending cold night. I'm instantly jealous of its innate sense, its call to action; when facing a fatherchallenge, I usually recoil into my infancy posture, unable to decide what to do—there are too many fucking choices. Being a good father is toggling the switch between self and selfless, until years later you realize it should have been stuck on the latter.

Re: the coyote. The only sense I have is to stab through its chest plate with a ringed key and remove its hide for my benefit. I have yet to understand why the human instinct is to kill, violate, and pillage; our greedy hearts beat within a fatty wall of shame. The animal then notices my head sprouting from the dirt and shows its teeth, as if it has smelled my thoughts. I always forget the damage caused by the images our minds paint. It steps toward me and snarls. To this I internally retreat and close my eyes to mimic prayer, the unifying signal of surrender.

It's here where I feel capable of true human silence, both inside and out. Finally, capable of listening. The fear of death will do it every time, a complete wiping out of the map of thought. An uninhibited awareness. Even if what I hear now in the sounds of the forest is indecipherable and terrifying, I can place myself within a system of being, an order in which I humbly accept not being first. This, I realize, is the point. To be a part of and to flow with; there is nothing to control. It is when I understand my place in this order, I can return to my family. Until then I listen and look for Jaden and Laney carrying shovels, signaling to them with my eyes just please don't let me die here; I promise to be better.

Consolations
of the Mask

Session #1, The Meeting

Gio is starting therapy again, but now, at twenty-six, fourteen years after his first time, he is seeing Cognitive Behavioral Therapist Dr. Barry Nobler. The office shares its waiting area with a hair salon next door, so while Gio fills out the questionnaire grading his symptoms, he tries to guess which of the messy haired, wild-eyed people around him are the insane, and which just need a haircut. The answers aren't as easy as he thought; turns out, at this hour, 7:45 a.m. on a Saturday morning, everyone looks kind of crazy, or unkempt.

> *On a scale of 1-5, how has your sleep been? (1 being the lowest in quality, 5 being the highest)*

1

If answered 1 or 2, please briefly explain why:

My dreams have become increasingly vivid.
And I now wake up multiple times in the night,
unsure of what's real and what's not.

Man talking to himself near watercooler on Bluetooth device—not insane. Woman making strange, contorted faces into phone—also not insane, just taking selfies. Man, constantly looking over shoulder at Gio—possibly insane. Gio—insane. Woman sitting quietly, softly flipping over the pages of her paperback—definitely insane.

Have you felt that you are not in control of your own ideas or thoughts? Yes or no.

Who can say if one is in control to begin with? To this, I answer: Where does thought originate? Am I thinker of my thoughts, or the observer? And where does control come into this? I, say for the purpose of control, I follow each thought as if it were a possum and I follow and follow it down into its dark den until it is trapped. Is this control? Or, say, I cannot follow the possum, it is too fast too blurry, and it spins me around knocks me to my knees, have I lost the control? Yes.

Dr. Barry Nobler finally calls Gio into his office. It is not what he expected—thick dusty carpet, small wooden desk facing the wall with piles of papers and no computer, a bright red retro floral couch with two golden dragon embroidered tufted throw pillows, and a green velvet armchair beside that. Gio sits on the couch, and reflexively puts one of the throw pillows on his lap, then consciously realizes this action may have indicated he is, on some level, feeling guarded, or turned off by the whole therapy gig. Which would be true if he weren't stoned. So, coolly, he slides the pillow far away from his crotch as possible, and then spreads his legs. Sitting back, he smacks his lips and says, "So, Dr. Nobler I—"

"Please, call me Barry."

Barry slides the chair forward; they are practically touching knees. Gio studies his face; he is surprisingly young looking. Green and white buffalo plaid shirt beneath a slim fitting V-neck sweater, a wide semi-wrinkled forehead, clean shaven with a wide chin, large square clear glasses, and an up-spouted mouth like a deep-sea bass.

"Well, Barry, I was hoping to not really do the whole 'let's start from the beginning' thing and just talk about what's going on right now."

"No time like the present. And I'm no Freudian! Why get Jung up on the past?"

"Right. All I'm saying is, I've been in therapy before."

"Is that so?" Barry asks, clicking his pen, putting ink to pad.

"Yup. Not going into it. I'm here to talk about my girlfriend."

Do things appear different from the way they usually do? (If yes, please explain.)

Things seem to have become less solid, lately. Images blur into other images, like the way wet paint runs on paper. I see streaks of light running toward then off to the side of my eyes. Typical when my glasses are dirty, which they are right now. So, no.

"You had some fun with the questionnaire, I see," Barry says.

"I have difficulty in answering questions, to be honest. There always seems to be a few answers to every question."

"Okay. So, try this one: Why are you here, Gio?"

"Here on the planet? Here in this life?"

"Here in this room, try."
"My girlfriend Valencia asked to meet my family."[2]

---

2 They were in bed when she asked; it was random and innocent, yet, damaging in ways she hardly knew. He lay still, breathing heavily through his mouth, hoping the unanswered question would fade away like a forgotten dream. Across the bedside wall, the sun was casting a shadow of the ladder bookshelf, leaving a dusty yellow veil over the books. Val snapped a picture with her phone. Gio watched her apply a black and white filter to the photo, add the caption **Morning Sun**, then post it to Instagram. It was artsy as hell. Gio liked this about her, her effortless way of sharing her artistic eye on social media. Where she seemed translucent through a screen, he came off as forced.

Gio was attracted to Val's Instagram account before he knew much about her. They met through friends at a bar, added each other as friends that night.

"Wow," Gio shouted over the bar's ambiance. He had just scrolled through her profile for a quick glance where he saw the horizon at dusk, a coffee in focus with a blurry skyline painted behind it, some acrylic smeared canvases placed in different settings, a bodega, a garden, a subway platform. "Are you like an artist or something?"

"Just an observer," she said, smiling into the foamy mouth of her beer.

Soon, he lived in anticipation of her next post. He found himself checking his phone more and more. Under the table at dinner, even at the urinal at work; he would obsessively check his phone and open Instagram before his thoughts began to shout at themselves. Stalker. Creep. It's ok. It's normal to be interested. She'll post. When she did post, he would not double tap right away, but casually, usually after a beer, and not within an hour of posting time. And with each new post he felt closer to her.

One day she messaged him for a book recommendation. Their first date was to the bookstore in Montclair, a store with levels and ladders full of books. Val had Instagrammed a picture of him in a cove of literary fiction with the caption **New and Exciting Men in Fiction.**

In bed, to be behind the scenes of her new post excited him. It was like an extra getting to work a scene with a famous actor. All that obsessive energy running through him; if she leaned over to touch him, he'd burst. After the photo was taken and posted, Val clicked off the screen of her phone and raised her arms to stretch. Gio pulled out his phone, opened Instagram to see her new post, then burrowed his head beneath the blanket to kiss Val's ribcage.

"Hey, hey," she said, squirming. "You didn't answer my question."

Gio pretended like he didn't hear, continuing to stamp his lips down to her hip. She flinched and dug her nails into his shoulders.

"Will you stop? I'm trying to have a conversation."

"What do you want me to say?" he said. "That I don't want you to meet my family?"

"What's the big deal? I've met your mom and dad."

Good point. But his parents weren't like the rest of his family. They were outliers. A duo who stubbornly survived through decades of witnessing the rest of the family's trauma, bipolar tendencies, substance addiction and abuse, to ease into their elderly years with their sanity and the knowledge of knowing who they would never be: them. Val didn't understand that to compare Gio's parents to his extended family was to compare the head of the iceberg to its glacial body beneath the surface. He considered a photo for such a caption. Perhaps snap

Barry bites down on the end of the pen and looks past Gio as if his next question is hanging on the wall behind him. Then, as he lifts his pad, seemingly preparing to write something about Gio's hesitancy to introduce Val to his family, he jolts up, groans, "Agh. Agh. Agh."

Gio jumps back, reflexively grabbing a dragon embroidered throw pillow and, yet again, jams it into his crotch.

"Pen busted in my mouth," Barry says through tight lips. Drooling, coughing, and stammering to his desk, Dr. Nobler then spits a black wad of ink into the trash. Gio watches it roll down a folded ramp of yellow legal pad,

---

Val's head of auburn hair rolling over the duvet with a slice of shoulder blade peeking out, hinting at the nude body beneath. No. Cliché, he thought and erased the post from his mind.

"I'm going to have to meet them someday, you know," she said. Another hint at marriage. Gio had noticed these lately, little slips implying their future together was certain. They've only been dating for nine months. Yet, the thought of spending the rest of his life with Val didn't scare him. Or did it? He's been lying to her, hasn't he? This guy, this well-mannered customer service representative who enjoys one beer here or there, who dozes off to sleep before ten and goes to the gym—it's all bullshit isn't it? It's not who he was before they started dating; it was someone he became. Like a polished selfie, he became what he thought she would like.

"It's just that they are different," he said, plunging under the blanket for one more deep-sea dive. Val resisted once more, sliding herself down to meet his eyes.

"Everyone has that crazy family member. I mean, you've met my uncle."

Ah, yes. Uncle Herbert. Val's PG13 version of the family's crazy uncle. Before they met, Val had properly warned him. "Whatever you do, don't talk politics," she said. Politics? Ha. Gio's uncle did politics the Hell's Angels way. "I think I'll be okay," he said. When Gio met Uncle Herbert, with his high-waisted khakis and Crocs, he thought, my uncle would eat your uncle. Medium Rare.

Gio was jealous of the closeness of Val's family, though. They spent every holiday together with rich traditions; they even got together for dinner every Sunday—and if you missed one week, you were sure as hell there the next week, on dish duty, Puto. Val held such an importance to family, each relative played a crucial role in developing the strong woman that she is. It was clear she wanted to see a likeness there in him. He wondered if it was a Puerto Rican thing. Italians held a similar responsibility to family, but with some teeth showing. A keep your enemies closer kind of thing.

"Fine," he said, lifting himself out of bed. He felt seasick. "Do you want to go to my aunt's next weekend? They're having some get together for my cousin. I think it's his birthday."

"Sure," she said. "And stop kissing my side—I hate that."

imagines the marbled stream as some sort of poison. From there, his mind does this spectacular leap to a time where he once saw an octopus shoot ink at his face and scurry across the bottom of the tank at the state zoo. Gio laughs to himself at Dr. Nobler's spastic motions of wiggly arms and quivery legs resembling the arms of that octopus, but without realizing, his laugh, the one that always got him in trouble in school, had projected across the room. Barry's head snatched back around, mouth stained with dried ink and spit, says, "You think that's funny huh?"

Circle yes or no, Do you find yourself laughing out of no-where, only to yourself?

If laughing comes from stimuli, albeit internal or external, what merit does such a question have? If I write yes, then, what? I, the insane laugh to myself. If no, I come across as having a flat affect, implying that one should entertain oneself, using memory as some projector casting reels of hilarity for the sole purpose of what? Reducing ennui? Passing time? Numbing oneself from suffering?

He apologizes and tells Barry that he has a certain tick, or habit; he can't help but blurt out in laughter at any human error, fall, mistake, etc. When Barry asks, "Do you consider yourself a perfectionist?" Gio blames it on hours and hours and hours of America's Home Video at a very impressionable age. Barry smiles, teeth black now, and writes this down. He looks at his watch.

"Sorry about that, I'll give you a free twenty minutes if you want to continue."

Gio agrees; he has nowhere to be.

"So, it's obvious there is some aversion to Val meeting your extended family, and I'd like to dig in here and really try to understand why. You must love Val and hate your family, or vice versa, which I doubt the latter. You're keeping one sacred, the other cursed. What about Val, or the family, seems incapable of reaching across and mending the other?"

Gio clenches the pillow and regrets coming off as shaken by this surface level observation. He must admit this guy is pretty good. But he swore to himself, he would not go into his trauma with this one. He would not get to the place he once found himself in, at the age 12, in the hands of another healthcare professional.

"You're hiding something, aren't you? How have you been sleeping? Any wild dreams?"[3]

Gio stretches, cranks his neck. "Let's pump the brakes, Doc. This is the first session. I don't know if I'm ready to dig that deep yet."

---

3 All week, after Val asked to meet his family, Gio dreamt of different scenarios in which various members of his family threw a burlap sack over his head and choked him with a rope. In one, his aunt Marianne held his head underwater in a bathtub until her cigarette burned through the filter. She said, "You're lucky I don't smoke 100's anymore," before he woke up.

Sleep-deprived and twitchy from caffeine, Gio called out of work that Friday to go on a solo hike to the reservoir nearby. He decided he would smoke a little pot, meditate, and flip through the collection of John Ashbery's poetry he'd been meaning to get around to. A solid day to decompress. More so a day to prepare himself for whatever the following week had in store for him and Val. He realized he knew what to expect. He was familiar with his family's antics; their addictions, their pettiness, their small crimes against any patriarchal views on what a family was supposed to be. He recognized that in himself, too. After all, he was an innocent bystander to it all through his adolescence, even a partaker in his early twenties. At one-point, smoking pot with his aunt in her garage, shot-gunning a beer with his uncle next to the grill, Gio referred to his family as "awesome," but now he saw them for what they were. Fucking toxic.

He wasn't sure if Val was ready to see that side of him: his dad's side, those who rip shots of tequila at a nine-year-old's birthday party and throw down vicious lines of spite and sometimes, depending on how much tequila consumed, get physical. Even worse than Val witnessing this firsthand, he knew his childhood would be out there for their disposal, every embarrassing memory could be presented to Val like a gift, saying: *Here, open it. This is who your boyfriend is.*

"Okay, no past, no depth. What do you want to talk about, Gio?"

"Octopuses."

Dr. Nobler looks at him over the bridge of his glasses. "What about them?"

"Each of their arms works independently. This prevents entanglement, but it makes me curious you know, like does their brain have overseeing power? What if one of the arms goes rogue, sabotages the other five arms? That has to be possible."

"Where, uh, where is this coming from, Gio?"

"…because I fear this, a lot actually. Like, what if part of my brain takes over the other parts of my brain? Like the amygdala, and I just become uncontrollably violent?"

"Do you have violent thoughts?

Do you have violent thoughts? If yes, on a scale of 1–5, please describe the intensity.

Violence in my mind is an unwanted house guest dirtying every dish, every mug, rubbing dirty shoes on carpet, doesn't flush, leaves— you get it. 5.

"Not more than anyone else. If anything, I kind of fear them, or detest them, so, like any crazy ex-boyfriend, they come back with more intensity, pounding on the door of my mind. Are you familiar with the Modular Mind Theory?"

Dr. Nobler runs a hand over his smooth chin, says, "I don't follow pop psychology," which makes Gio feel like he doesn't understand him. Gio hates to be understood. Still with the throw pillow over his crotch, he leans forward, says, "That came out wrong. I do that a lot. I just ramble sometimes, like in vortexed loops, getting deeper as the thoughts go around."

"I see. Do you have any coping skills?"

"Like an ability to cope?"

When Gio hears the word cope, he thinks of the years from sixteen to twenty-two, spending most of his time in dim basements getting wrecked with his friends. He is clean now—well, California clean, just pot—but not clean from the addict mind that dictates every thought, every feeling, every action. It gnaws at him, or who he perceives himself to be, a victim to this addict brain. He once read about the "Self" and how, when put under a thought microscope, it is hard to pin down. That comforted him, picturing his "true" self somewhere floating on the outside of his malfunctioning brain, an innocent onlooker.

"I mean, do you have things you like to do, that, err, helps you not get stuck in those vortexed loops, as you call it."

"I like going to the reservoir."[4]

---

[4] At the reservoir that day, Gio couldn't escape the feeling that Val was sure to dump him after she saw who his family was. Better yet, who he was. Whatever happened at the barbecue was up for interrogation, all could be brought forth by the defense that deep down he is one of them, a selfish, shitty person. That's what he saw addiction as now, just some sort of selfish need to be fulfilled. With each drug he would try, his focus would shift inward, and he would lose sight of everything around him. The same went for his family, it was like they wore masks with the inner lining of mirrors, incapable of seeing outside of themselves, with nothing but a plain construct to offer everyone else.

He wondered how many times he could apply a new mask over himself to create someone new. Maybe that's why he rarely posted to Instagram and Val did constantly. Social media platforms should be an extension of your true self. He struggled with this, always posting then deleting a photo in place of another, with each layer and alteration covering something up; the pain, the shame, the truth. There was something in him that believed the more he did this, the closer he would get to becoming that creation of himself. But Val's love for him—and views of family—cut right through and exposed it for the fallacy that it was. She deserved better.

At the reservoir, he sat on a flat rock near the edge of a small cliff overlooking the water. He scanned the landscape to make sure he was alone in nature then sparked the end of a joint. He held the heavy smoke in his chest and focused on holding his breath. He let his thoughts pass by with the breeze rolling through the scatter of leaves. His smoky breath emitted out as the leaves tumbled over each other. Just as he was about to close his eyes, he heard splashing in the distance; a heron had lifted itself onto a log in the center of the reservoir and nestled itself beside two turtles. The turtles laid back on each other, balancing themselves on the log

"Nature is one of the best healers, that's good."

To Gio, Dr. Nobler seems to be one of those late boomers that were babies during Vietnam but grew up with the impression of its corruption pressed into their brains; that, by the time they were teenagers, the only way they knew how to channel this protest was to take on full blown nihilism, narcissism, and stubbornness, and throw themselves into subterranean culture with the snobbish air of aristocrats. No music was better. No art was better. It all showed through Barry's perfectly trimmed hair to give off the illusion of being unkempt. He wears Converses and the first thing he said to Gio was, "What's up, man?"

Dr. Nobler goes on, "I don't know if you know this about trees but it's like the philosophical question, 'Does God need humans to exist?' and vice versa. Apply this to our relation to trees, exchanging carbon dioxide for oxygen, and see that the spiritual connection from us to nature is in the breath. The closer you are to the breath, the closer you are to 'God.'"

"I don't believe in God."

Barry stammers, "No, I know, well I don't know, I didn't mean to imply that, but it was a simile, a metaphor, an aphorism—doh."

Do you have strong feelings or beliefs about being unusually gifted or talented in some way?

I do believe that I'm meant to do great things. Now how this applies to my state of mental health, I'm not sure. Motivation, goals, aspiration, self-confidence— these are bad things?

as the heron spread its wings, getting comfortable on the opposite end. Gio slid out his phone, snapped a picture, and uploaded it to Instagram. The caption read like the beginning of a bad joke: **Two turtles and a heron meet on a log**, right… He deleted the post a few minutes later, before he hiked back to his car.

There is an awkward pause between he and Barry. Gio checks the clock on the wall above the closed door. He has another fifteen minutes.

"God aside, Gio, you know we need to talk about your past a little bit, right? To figure out what's going on between you and your girlfriend, we need to at least lay some groundwork here."

"It's not about what's going on between us, it's that she really wants to meet my extended family. It like, would solidify something for her or something, give her the whole picture."

"And you feel an aversion to this? To her meeting your family or taking the relationship to the next step?"

"Her meeting the family."

Gio's fingers dig into the throw pillow. He feels the raised stitching of the dragons slide beneath his nails and with it, their fire trickles in-between his skin and muscle, igniting heat and sweat throughout his body. Dr. Nobler seems to notice, but rather than embarrass him by asking if he is hot or if something is wrong, he asks, "What about meeting the family is preventing you from introducing her?"

Gio's heart is a speed bag. His mind swirls with images blurring together; if you could pluck one picture from this zoetrope, a single image would appear: his uncle.

"I was sexually abused as a child, by, um, my uncle."

Dr. Nobler's face shows no expression; his eyes are just steady lenses focusing, zooming in to analyze him a little closer.

"I'm sorry this happened to you. Is this why you saw a therapist when you were younger?"

"Yeah, Dr. Gorski."[5]

Dr. Nobler keeps his eyes on Gio, then slides him a tissue box.

"It's okay, I'm actually kind of over it. Dr. Gorski really helped me. He was a bit of a kook, from what I remember, but he really helped put everything into context. My abuse. My anger. My depression."

"But yet, you continue to suffer?"

"Hmm. I never thought of it like that."

Have you heard unusual sounds like banging, clicking, hissing, clapping or ringing in your ears?

I believe there to be another plane of reality that exists right before our eyes, unseen to our limited perception but bridged through sound. There is no other explanation for the phenomena of hearing your name called when no one is there, being awoken by a loud clap on the inside of the ears, etc.

---

5 Dr. Donovan Gorski was not the average psychiatrist; he specialized in hypno-therapy, a practice shunned by the psychology community. Every session was two hours long, where the patient would be under hypnosis for an hour and a half, with a fifteen-minute briefing at the start and debriefing at the end. Dr. Gorski invented a special practice in which he called "Analyzation of Self" where the patient would wear various masks throughout the hypnotism; the masks represented different forms of the personality and under the guide of the therapist, the patient confronts any part of themselves where they find trouble.

Gio saw Dr. Gorski for two years; his dad found him through an ad online. He felt it would help for Gio to have someone to talk to about his random outbursts of anger, depression, and his tentative sleepwalking.

"Addicted to addiction? Shackled by grief? By Trauma?" The ad said. "Click to break the chain."

After the first session, Gio was hooked. He felt his mind become softer, his attitude, lighter. The second session revealed something about Gio that he never saw coming. In a hypnotic state, Dr. Gorski presented Gio with the idea that he was sexually abused as a child. It wasn't long before Gio could piece together fragments of memory, until the trauma was clear, and more like reality than any memory he's ever had. This gave context beneath his addictive personality, his anger, and his disdain for not just his Uncle Paul, but the rest of the extended family, whom he considered bystanders.

"So, this can get a little murky. You know, Client/ patient privilege and such. But, do you want to talk about Dr. Gorski's practices? You seem pretty...pretty stricken, or reluctant with him. You kind of tensed up a bit when you said his name."

"I can't remember much. I'm pretty sure he would hypnotize me."

Dr. Nobler scratches his chin and squints. Before he says something, perhaps an opinion on the act of hypnotizing, the alarm clock on his desk chimes.

"Ah, out of time for today. What do you say we pick this up next week? I'd like to see you again, Gio."

"Sure," Gio says, releasing the throw pillow, and standing to meet Barry's extended hand for a shake.

> *Do you have a history of seizures, head trauma, headaches, or anything that would prevent a brain scan?*

No.

Session #2, The Scan

The hair salon is closed on Tuesdays; there's no one around for Gio to project his worry onto. That sometimes is the best part of his down time, balling up his worry and tossing it in the face of someone close by. When he releases it, it becomes something new—anger, depression, jealousy—it doesn't matter, as long as he was free of it. But sitting there, sun at his back, flipping through the worn-out pages of book titled *Cabin Porn*, waiting for Val to text him back, he feels his worry hang around, and dig in deeper to stay. She isn't texting him back, which a thought at the back of Gio's mind says, "Good. Problem solved."

But to that he says, "Shut up." Did he say that out loud? When there is no one else in the waiting area for a psychiatrist's office to compare your level of crazy to, you know what you are. Despite a notion of will power, or what Dr. Gorski would call "your iron mask" which means your strongest sense of self, Gio texts Val: i'm sorry about Friday night.[6]

---

6 Friday, date night. His night to pick. He chose a tapas place that served their beers in odd-shaped beakers and their cocktails in gold-rimmed jars. The place was dimly lit and named "Bent Spoon." Over each table were hollowed out paint cans filled with small tinted blue flames that hung from the ceiling on rope. Val was eating that shit up—beaming with a drunken glow, like the night they first met.

If only that smile would last, Gio thought. They were a week away from the party. He hasn't even told her about the things she might see or hear. He had intended to tell her everything—about his family, about his past—before the tiny pork belly sliders got to the table, but the next thing he knew he was inhaling one honey whiskey after the other watching his breath freeze on the glass as his mouth hovered over the ice. He didn't expect to get so drunk. This was the time to debrief Val, to come clean, and warn her of the day to come. His thoughts were screaming, I'm a fraud. I'm a liar. Don't trust me. Instead, he chose to suppress those thoughts behind the mask of alcohol. After each drink, he slurped drops of honey whiskey off the large ball of ice buoying in his glass, hoping the waiter would hear the international call for a refill. Steadying his eyes on Val helped, sort of.

"What are you smiling about?" she asked, playfully slanting her lips. And what was he smiling about? Yes, Val looked ravishing in a low strung blue blouse, but it was not the time to swoon.

"I'm just… happy," he said.

"You're drunk."

"What's the difference?"

He reached out and touched her hand. He thought about pulling out his phone and taking a picture, but he just focused his eyes on hers and blinked, hoping that the image would seep into his mind for good. Hashtag: no filter.

They walked up Main Street afterward, Val with her hands tucked in the pockets of her pea coat. It was cold. Gio was walking with boozy confidence—denim jacket open, breath swelling into smoke.

"Let's not go to the party," he said. "Fuck it."

"What? Why not?"

And why not? The way he was avoiding it made him seem like the problem to Val, and not his family. Sometimes the hardest image to face is the one looking back at you in a mirror. He had his uncle's laugh, his aunt's nose, their smiles. All of it was ingrained in him; and how easy it was to tap into. Easy as drinking five whiskeys with dinner. He could already see himself picking up his old habits, the smoking, binge drinking, the drugs, harassing women. It was all there festering inside of him behind each mask he wore, making the muscles in his arm twitch.

"I don't know. I just don't think you'll have a good time."

"Meeting family is not about having a good time, Val said. "But it's nice to meet the people who helped raise you. I wanna know where you come from."

"True North Cabin, Copper Harbor, Michigan"

"Nestled into the rocky shoreline of Lake Superior and faces directly north—a perfect vantage point for the Northern Lights. It was designed in the 1960s using exclusively self-chopped wood, cut in the traditional right moon sign. Painted red to symbolize energy, passion, desire. This cabin shows your teeth, releases your inner wolf."

Gross, Gio thinks. Not pictured: Two old hippies who want to watch you bathe. He tosses the thick hardcover book back onto the leather ottoman in front of his chair. Just then, a woman enters the waiting area from the door of the hair salon. She is older, hunched, with bright orange hair and leopard print leggings, holding a 3 lb. bag of ground coffee. Angel on earth. Gio looks up. Sun catches his retinas. Squints.

"You want decaf or regular, hon." Reg-ah-la.

"The hard stuff, please."

The woman dumps ground coffee into a large plastic filter and drops it into the top of a coffee maker that looks like the tower of an old computer. It starts to whizz and hiss, and gurgle water. The woman walks over and knocks on the door to Dr. Nobler's office, announces, "Barry, ya patient is out here." She turns to Gio. "Help ya self,"

"No you don't," he said. He swiped away his hand from hers and felt the urge to break free. He wanted to run, to cross the street, out of line of streetlamps that were guiding them home and find a place in the woods where he would rip out any pieces of his family that remained in him and bury them beneath the pines. To then return to Val bloodied, but new, with no evidence of where he came from but only wounds to be scarred over and forgotten.

For the rest of the night Val was silent. They walked next to each other, but individually, like strangers, until they got to Val's apartment where she said, "I'll text you," before leaving Gio at the door.

which Gio isn't sure whether she meant to the coffee or to use the practice of therapy to help himself. His thoughts ask, "Could one supplement the other? If he were cured of whatever his ailments, could he no longer have to depend on his vices?" Maybe that's what being "cured" is—capable to deal with life and all its shit and stay sober while doing it.

Eventually, Dr. Nobler calls Gio into his office and after apologizing for the wait, he guides him to sit at the couch where there is a packet of forms and a pen on the coffee table between them.

"So, today's session is going to work a little different," Dr. Nobler says. "We're going to do a 15-minute session, then we will go into the next room for an EEG scan, followed by another 15–20-minute session."

Gio says okay, and then asks why the EEG scan is necessary.

"Well, I want to really get inside your head," he says, chuckling slightly. "For the lack of a better phrase. But it seems to me that you clearly have some repressed trauma and somehow, one way or another, your former psychiatrist Dr. Uh. Dr.—"

"Gorski."

"Right, Dr. Gorski, is an intricate part of it. And through brain scan imaging and thorough questioning, I will be able to parse out what goes with what. It's all very advanced. Do you understand?"

"No, not really," Gio says, sitting back, considering grabbing the dragon embroidered throw pillow.

"Basically, without getting too scientific here, you will answer a series of questions. Some will be random to establish a base of your memory. Like, 'What is your favorite memory from one of your birthdays?' While you think of this memory, the scan will show a map of your brain lighting up in certain ways. Then, we'll get to questions regarding your trauma and your sessions with Dr. Gorski and compare the results."

"And those will look different?"

"Actually, hopefully not. We want those images to be as similar as we can get, because that would mean your brain no longer associates your trauma with negative emotion. That would be major, and—if I'm being honest with you—a huge breakthrough. And, telling you right now, would probably mean there's no reason for you to continue therapy."

"Okay, but what about the reason why I came here in the first place? To talk about my girlfriend?"

"Well, I'm under the assumption that these two things are connected. That your trauma is preventing you from making progress in your relationships. So, let's say the image of your brain while discussing the trauma lights up like a god-darn Christmas tree, then we have a fine place to start."

Gio nods, puts his hands together, and says, "Well, all right," then picks up the pen to start reviewing the paperwork.

#

The headgear for the EEG scan is cold and smells like burnt rubber. It sits on his head like a helmet with rows of wires sprouting out in all directions and running down his side and back, all connecting to a computer-like screen where Dr. Nobler sits behind. Gio feels like a villain in a comic book movie, that through the power of thought and electricity he could take over the world.

"Okay, Gio. Let's begin. Please picture the color yellow, as if the inside of your head is filled with yellow."

Gio does. The machine beeps and ticks.

"Now red, please."

Gio does. The machine beeps and ticks.

"Okay, now black."

Gio does. The machine beeps and ticks.

"Good. Good. Okay, now try to picture some images from your childhood that make you feel nostalgic.

Gio does. A wooden gate with a latch that gets jammed. A broken trampoline hovering over dead grass. An above-ground pool in the far corner of the yard with decaying vinyl walls and green water. These are things Gio would always remember about his Aunt Darlene's backyard. They are always in the background of his memories, flickering like old VHS camera footage of his childhood. The trampoline. That's where he used to have flipping contests with his cousin Sal, before the overdose. The pool. Where his cousins Giana and Ricky would throw him in with all his clothes on. In the house, popcorn ceilings, a plaid couch, an oversized entertainment center stocked with stereo equipment, a VHS player, and dusted over CD cases stacked neatly in a plastic rack, some scattered under the TV with their cover sleeves missing. The wood paneled walls of the living room with three slats missing from when Uncle Paul threw Linda into it.

"Whoa, nice, Gio," Dr. Gorski says, looking intently into the monitor. "Okay, I'd like for you to remember your trauma, as best you can. And if you feel your anxiety start to rise, it's okay to stop. I'm here with you."

Gio does and sees the living room in his head, the same as it was in session with Dr. Gorski under hypnosis. He's alone. The sun casts a beam of dust onto the wall. Tree branches tap the window. His uncle enters—tall, thin, and tan with a thick white mustache. The TV is on. His uncle lays on the couch; his jeans rise and tighten around his thighs, his crotch. Some more details start to become clear, ones that he doesn't ever remember having. A baseball game is on. Yankees vs. Padres. It is the fifth inning. He sees the camera roll over the crowd. His uncle cracks a beer. All new details. His uncle then waves him over, mouths the words, "Come lie down. Come over here." His anxiety starts to increase. He feels his heartbeat thumping in his neck and ears, like it's smacking against the inside of the EEG helmet. This part is where Dr. Gorski would guide him through, tell him what he sees and feels, but now, in his own memory, the images start to blur and break apart; it feels as if he could fill them with whatever he wants to make them feel whole again. This is when, under hypnosis, he would yell, "This isn't real!" But Dr. Gorski would urge that it was, that it is. Here, now, in his head, the further he falls into this pool of memory, the more abstract it gets. He tries to concentrate on the images he always saw with Dr. Gorski, but the closer he looks into them, the more they feel movie-like, like his memory was shot from an eagle-eye point of view. He tries to maintain the viewpoint of his own eyes. He sees his uncle, now next to him on the couch, keeping his hands to himself, earnestly watching the game. That's it. His dad gets home. They all watch the game together. He doesn't know what to believe. He can no longer tell which one the real memory is.

Back on the couch, Gio is clenching the dragon-embroidered pillow, Dr. Nobler tells him that the scan went great, that he thinks he got what he needed. After some standard questions to assess Gio's anxiety level, he tells him that he will call him back in by Friday with the results, which happens to be the day before Val's is going to meet his family.

---

7 While Gio was getting the EEG scan, he received two text messages from Val. One said to not worry about getting drunk and kind of sloppy. The other text said not to worry so much about

Session #3, Friday

With the family party tomorrow, Gio feels somewhat high-strung, as if he had drunk three large coffees on the way to Dr. Nobler's office. He gets to his ten o'clock appointment on time, despite the rain and slow-moving trucks on Rt. 76[8], and Dr. Nobler is waiting in his office with the door open, wearing a Queens of the Stone Age band t-shirt and brown tinted jeans.

"Casual Fridays," he says, smiling, then directs Gio to come in and sit down.

Gio sits in his usual spot between the two dragon embroidered throw pillows. On the coffee table, he notices a manila envelope with his name on it. After answering a few routine questions—like how he is feeling, how has been sleeping, etc.—Gio is too distracted by the folder to continue. He wants to know the results of the EEG scan, and Dr. Nobler seems

---

her meeting his family, that regardless of who they are or what they have done, she is in a relationship with him, not them. This made Gio feel somewhat positive. He felt that her stable psyche and confidence in her moral judgment could make decisions for them both, and that maybe if he just trusted her instincts, he would not need to attend therapy anymore.

8 It was on Rt. 76 where Gio first told Val that he loved her. They were stopped in traffic, a pop ballad was playing on the radio, and Val, who was driving, reached across to put her hand on his thigh. This would have been the ultimate cliché scene had a guy in a F-150 pickup truck not then lay on the horn and give Val the finger as he pulled around her, to which she yelled, "Shit head!" Gio laughed, then Val had laughed because he had laughed, and soon they were both cracking up and it was then where the words, "I love you," spilled out of his mouth, leaving Val to say, "What did you say?" and Gio confirmed it to her, and in repeating it, he was able to convince himself that for the first time in his life he had felt something for someone else. When asked later what made him say that, he said to Val, "I guess I didn't want to go another second keeping that secret from you." And in that moment, it felt that he could be entirely himself with her, that nothing else mattered after he said those words. The next day, in bed, was when Val asked to meet his family.

to be toying with this fact by dragging out his words, elongating his responses, and sitting back in his chair with an air of smugness that signals to Gio that he is in no rush. Just as Gio is about to grab one of the dragon embroidered throw pillows and jam it into his crotch, Dr. Nobler says, "What do you say we go over your test?"

Gio leaves the pillow be and says, "Sure," as Dr. Nobler removes the photos of Gio's brain and lines them up on the coffee table like a hopscotch board in front of him. Dr. Nobler flicks a switch on a leg of the table and the center glows, illuminating the photos, and says, "You thought that was just a coffee table, huh?" Gio snickers. All the photos show a side view of a cashew shaped brain set in a blue skull outline against a black background. In some of the photos the coils of the brain tissue are blue with gray stems interconnecting throughout. In others, especially one—the bottom box of hopscotch—Gio notices how most parts of it are lit up in light green, orange and red.

"What you are looking at here is your brain activity during your memories," Dr. Nobler says. "I'm sure you could guess which ones are the happy memories and which ones are not." He takes the back of a pen and taps on the photo closest to him and the two underneath it. "These are when you thought of colors." Gio sees no difference in the color mapping. "And this one," he says, pointing at the single photo in the third row. "This one is when I asked you to think of something nostalgic." Two sections, like wings in the center of the brain are lit up bright green with swaths of red mixed in. "Now this is when it gets interesting," he says, pointing at the last two photos. Gio stares at them, failing to understand what he is looking at; they both have large pools of mixing colors, more so than any of the other ones combined. The only difference is, one's coloration shows at the front and the other at the dividing center line of the brain. "On the left here," Dr. Nobler says, pointing to the one with the coloration near the center, "is when I asked you to think of Dr. Gorski, and how I said to just picture his face and your hypnosis therapy. Your brain is showing major reaction to this. Deep and darker colors represent blood flow in this area, so during this time, your memory was being flooded with all sorts of emotion and stress. But this other one, when I asked you to think of your trauma, is lit up in the front here, in a space away from memory, and more toward familiarity."

Gio's face is blank.

"I know it sounds like a bunch of science mumbo jumbo, but do you know what this means?"

"No."

"This means that, one, your memory of Dr. Gorski is more traumatic than the memory of your quote-unquote trauma itself. Which is, uh, not likely. But it got me thinking." He is standing now, looking over the photos and Gio, like a king upon his seated nobleman. Gio grabs the dragon embroidered throw pillow and jams it in his crotch. "I couldn't stop thinking about how the activity for both are in two different areas of the brain, which made me realize it is possible that your trauma was totally fabricated."

"What?"

"Sounds crazy, I know, but it is possible. I've heard of this. Read about it in some journals online, saw it on Dr. Phil. People living with fake memories. And who else better than to do it than a hypnotist? Ha!"

Gio says, "So, let me get this straight.[9] I was never assaulted by my uncle?"

"Can't say for sure, but according to these tests, I would say

---

[9] Gio once thought about what the chances were that he was never abused. It was a few years ago, before he met Val. He sat up in bed one night, sweating at three o'clock in the morning considering the possibility he was lied to by Dr. Gorski. But the images were always so real and intense, causing full body sensations. That couldn't be faked right?

that it is highly unlikely. Actually, more likely that Dr. Gorski 'implanted' the memory than it being true. I say implanted here lightly, I don't want to imply some spy movie plot element. But it's more likely he uses this tactic to generate more business."

Gio slams the dragon embroidered throw pillow onto the couch and covers his face with his hands. Dr. Nobler slides over a box of tissues and says, "I'm here when you're ready to talk."

#

Right before the end of the session, Gio shows his face; it is swollen and bright red like raw meat. Dr. Nobler removes the gnawed pen from his mouth and offers some extra time. Gio nods in agreement then sits back.

"You know how when you know something to be true, you kind of feel it, physically?" Gio asks.

"I do, yes."

"Well, I kind of felt something was a little off about all of it. But it was like, it also made sense, you know? Like if my life was a math problem, you could easily sketch out that all my behaviors, emotions, thoughts, and actions would add up to having experienced some trauma."

"Well, to be clear, Gio. You have experienced trauma, a great deal of it. And maybe not in the way that you thought, but you still have experienced it. In some ways, we all have. That's what connects us. And it is not through the masks that we wear that binds us to one another. It is by showing the world what's underneath. To be open and honest about our suffering."

Gio stands up and exclaims, "But you don't know for sure if it happened or not."

"My point exactly. You will have to accept either as a possibility and understand that your trauma does not define you, and if you learn to live that truth, you will be more compassionate, empathetic, and kinder to all people, especially yourself. Then you will see that your vices are less controlling, and you become more honest with other people."

"But how doesn't it matter?" Gio asks. "How could I ever forgive my uncle if he did that?"

"That's a big 'if' there. But the right place to start is blind forgiveness, which has many facets. I call it blind because you'll learn that forgiving an abuser is about yourself and how it frees you, rather than letting them off the hook."

Gio squints and tosses this idea back and forth in his head. He's never thought about how stunted he was; that he rightfully held on to grief, anger, sadness, and apathy, using drugs to numb those emotions, rather than working through them to get to a place of openness. And that if this did happen to him, why should his uncle be out there able to live his life how he wants while Gio remained stuck in that place.

The small alarm clock on the coffee table goes off.

"So, where do I go from here?" Gio asks.

"Forward. You make amends with yourself then with everyone else. Tell your girlfriend, your uncle, and we'll work through this together."

"Okay," Gio says.

"Okay," Dr. Nobler says, smiling. "I'll see you next week."

In the car on his way to Val's, Gio takes the backroads off Rt. 76. The rain cleared up, letting the sun crack through the slabs of gray clouds as they drift apart. He passes a farm with a large blue barn sitting on a hill and an old airfield across from it on his right, where a tour group is getting ready to go sky diving. He pulls off to the side of the road and looks at each one of the people huddled around the instructor. There are three women and two men, all in full gear nodding in unison to whatever the small man in the center has to say to them. Gio briefly considers how each of them has had at least one traumatic experience in their lives, yet they're about to jump out of an airplane. He decides to pull out his phone and capture a picture of the way the group is standing just on the border of light, as if on stage, away from the shadow cast by the steel sheeted airport terminal; the big oaks in the background reach upward in a heap of emerald until being overcame by the vast blue of the fresh post-storm sky, all making the bright colors of the diver's suits (red, yellow, and orange) pop in the foreground. He confidently posts the photo to Instagram with the caption: Beautiful day to take the leap.

As the divers check their packs and one by one load onto the plane, his head is full of Dr. Nobler's kind and warm voice explaining how memory can be quite murky and unreliable and how we must accept our past regardless. Gio sees Val in his thoughts[10] and feels ready to tell her everything.

Now, Gio leans against the hood of his car and the plane containing the divers is up in the air; he hangs around until he can no longer see them overhead. He doesn't need to see them dive or land safely because when he gets back in his car and drives away, feeling a slight cold breeze on his face, he knows each of them will jump and scream and cry and laugh the entire way down until one day, looking back, they will smile when they tell the story of how they did one thing that terrified them.

---

[10] Usually when Val comes to mind he sees her from an extremely close point of view, like when she is right in his face when they are in bed, and he can look into the pores of her skin or the fraction of an inch between the hairs of her bangs, and light and skin and hair all paint this image as her lips press on his right after she says the words, "It will all be okay."

Acknowledgments

My thanks to David, Julia, and Josh at word west

for their belief, thought, and hard work behind this book, making it substantially better than I could have ever imagined. Thank you to my teacher Ben Obler. Thank you to Scott Zagorski, who reads everything I write, for what reason I have yet to understand, maybe you're a masochist, but your friendship, insight, and generosity are invaluable. Thank you to the writers and editors who have taken me in, shown support, or read an early draft of these stories, especially Dave Housely and the rest of *Barrelhouse*. Thank you to my first "first reader" Irene Pappas, my first "fan" Sheridan Tennant, Chris Pappas, Steve Krutz, Drs. Laura and Marty Frank, my parents, my sister Melissa, Arlene and Emil Schneider, thank you all for your love and support.
And thank you to Y—for everything & more.

Lightning Source UK Ltd.
Milton Keynes UK
UKHW010206070223
416581UK00020B/741/J